Close enough to feel the warmth of his body radiating in the space between them. Close enough to see the deep golden flecks in his brown eyes. "I haven't done anything yet," she said.

"You're here. Right now, that's everything."

Even though Jane was waking up and starting to fuss at still being swaddled in the blanket, Trish couldn't pull away from the way Nate's eyes held hers.

"You don't have to buy me a phone." It came out as a whisper.

The corner of his mouth curved up and he suddenly looked very much like a man who would seduce his temporary nanny just because he could. "And yet, I'm going to anyway."

Trish swallowed down the tingling sensation in the back of her throat. This was Nate after a nap? What would he be like after a solid night's sleep?

And how the hell was she going to resist him?

* * *

The Nanny Plan
is part of the #1 bestselling series
from Harlequin Desire:
Billionaires and Babies—Powerful men...
wrapped around their babies' little fingers.

* * *

If you're on Twitter,
tell us what you think of Harlequin Desire!
#harlequindesire

Dear Reader,

This is a story that started with a real-life event. Maggie Dunne, founder of Lakota Children's Enrichment, won a $20,000 award from *Glamour* magazine's 2012 Top Ten College Women contest. When Sir Richard Branson arrived to give a talk at her college a few weeks later, Maggie stood up with her large check and asked how to use the prize money to encourage celebrities to donate. Sir Branson matched her donation!

The idea of boxing one of the richest men in the world into a charitable corner—with a large check!— fascinated me. Inspired by both Maggie's boldness as well as the good work she does to promote education among the Lakota tribes, I decided to use her large-check moment as the opener for a novel.

The rest of the story is entirely fictional, it should be noted. Trish and Nate are entirely figments of my imagination and I hope you love them and baby Jane as much as I do!

The Nanny Plan is a sensual story about fighting for your dreams and falling in love. And if you'd like to find out more about the charity that inspired Trish's charity, please check out Lakota Children's Enrichment at lakotachildren.org. They're always accepting donations. Be sure to stop by sarahmanderson.com, and sign up for my newsletter at eepurl.com/nv39b to join me as I say long live cowboys!

Sarah M. Anderson

THE NANNY PLAN

SARAH M. ANDERSON

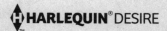

Recycling programs
for this product may
not exist in your area.

ISBN-13: 978-0-373-73379-8

The Nanny Plan

Copyright © 2015 by Sarah M. Anderson

Printed in U.S.A.

Award-winning author **Sarah M. Anderson** may live east of the Mississippi River, but her heart lies out West on the Great Plains. With a lifelong love of horses and two history teachers for parents, she had plenty of encouragement to learn everything she could about the tribes of the Great Plains.

When she started writing, it wasn't long before her characters found themselves out in South Dakota among the Lakota Sioux. She loves to put people from two different worlds into new situations and to see how their backgrounds and cultures take them someplace they never thought they'd go.

Sarah's book *A Man of Privilege* won the 2012 RT Reviewers' Choice Award for Best Harlequin Desire. Her book *Straddling the Line* was named Best Harlequin Desire of 2013 by *CataRomance*, and *Mystic Cowboy* was a 2014 Booksellers' Best Award finalist in the Single Title category as well as a finalist for the Gayle Wilson Award for Excellence.

When not helping out at her son's school or walking her rescue dogs, Sarah spends her days having conversations with imaginary cowboys and American Indians, all of which is surprisingly well tolerated by her wonderful husband. Readers can find out more about Sarah's love of cowboys and Indians at sarahmanderson.com.

Books by Sarah M. Anderson

HARLEQUIN DESIRE
The Nanny Plan

The Bolton Brothers
Straddling the Line
Bringing Home the Bachelor
Expecting a Bolton Baby

The Beaumont Heirs
Not the Boss's Baby
Tempted by a Cowboy
A Beaumont Christmas

Visit the Author Profile page
at Harlequin.com for more titles.

To Maggie Dunne, the founder of
Lakota Children's Enrichment.
You had a very large check and a whole lot of
gumption! While I changed many things,
I hope I kept your spirit of charitable action going!

To Maisey Yates and Jules Bennett,
who came up with the baby for this book.
You guys are the baby experts!

And to Laurel Levy for making sure I got the details
of San Francisco right. I'll get back out there
to visit you someday!

One

The auditorium was filling up, which was exactly what Trish wanted. Maybe four hundred people had crowded into the lower level and, in addition to the journalists from the college paper, some reporters from the San Francisco television stations were in attendance. Excellent. A good crowd would leverage some social pressure on her target. No billionaire would risk looking heartless by saying no to a charity in front of a big crowd.

Trish had been sitting in her spot—end of the third row, to the left of the podium on the stage—for over an hour. She'd gotten here early enough that no one had seen her smuggle in the check. She wished she could afford a cell phone—then she could at least play with that until the talk started instead of being the only person in the room who wasn't connected.

She was as ready as she was ever going to be. She just had to wait for her moment. Timing an ambush of one of the wealthiest men on the planet required precision.

Trish had planned everything down to her shirt—a great find at Goodwill. It was a distressed blue T-shirt with a vintage-looking Wonder Woman logo emblazoned over her breasts. It was a half size too small, but she had on her black velvet suit jacket, so it looked fine. Polished, with a geeky air.

Exactly like her target, Nate Longmire.

People continued to filter in for another thirty minutes. Everyone was here to see Longmire, the newest billionaire to come out of Silicon Valley's wealth generators. Trish had done her homework. Longmire was twenty-eight, which didn't exactly make him the "Boy Billionaire" that the press made him out to be. As far as Trish could tell, there wasn't anything particularly boyish about him.

He was six foot two, broadly built and according to her internet searches, single. But the plan wasn't to hit on him. The plan was to make him feel like she was a kindred soul in all things nerd—and all things compassionate. The plan was to box him into a corner he could only donate himself out of.

Finally, the lights in the auditorium dimmed and the president of the Student Activities Board came out in a remarkably tight skirt. Trish snorted.

"Welcome to the Speaker Symposium at San Francisco State University. I am your host, Jennifer McElwain..."

Trish tuned the woman out as Jennifer went on about SFSU's "long and proud" history of social programming, other "distinguished guests," blah-blah. Instead of listening, Trish scanned the crowd. Over half of the mostly female crowd looked like they were hoping for a wild ride in a limo to happen within an hour.

The sight of so many young, beautiful women made Trish feel uneasy. This was not her world, this college full of young, beautiful people who could casually hook up and hang out without worrying about an unexpected pregnancy, much less how to feed that baby. Trish's world was one of abject poverty, of never-ending babies that no one planned for and, therefore, no one cared for. No one except her.

Not for the first time, she felt like an interloper. Even though she was in her final year of getting a master's degree in social work—even though she'd been on this campus for five years—she still knew this wasn't her world.

Suck it up, she thought to herself as she counted the number of television cameras rolling. Five. The event was getting great press.

She was a woman with a large check and a second-hand Wonder Woman T-shirt waiting to ambush one of the richest men on the planet. That was her, Trish Hunter, in a nutshell.

"...And so," Jennifer went on, "we are thrilled to have the creator of SnAppShot, Mr. Nate Longmire, here with us tonight to discuss social responsibility and the Giving Pledge!"

The crowd erupted into something that wasn't quite a cheer but came damn close to a catcall as the Boy Billionaire himself walked on stage.

The audience surged to their feet and Trish surged with them. Longmire walked right past her. She had an excellent view of him.

Oh. Oh, *wow*. It's not like she didn't know what Nate Longmire looked like. She'd read up on his public persona—including that ridiculous article naming him one of the Top Ten Bachelors of Silicon Valley, complete with a photo spread.

But none of the pictures—not a single one of them—did the man justice. Attraction spiked through her as she studied him. In person, the tall frame and the broad shoulders weren't just eye-catching, they moved with a rippled grace that left her feeling flushed. He had on hipster jeans and Fluevog boots, but he'd paired them with a white tailored shirt with French cuffs and a purple sweater. A striped purple tie was expertly tied around his neck. He wore a scruffy beard and thick horn-rimmed glasses. They were the nerdiest things about him.

Longmire turned his face to the crowd and Trish swore

she saw him blush as the thunderous noise continued. He did not preen. If anything, he looked almost uncomfortable. Like he didn't quite fit in up there.

"Thank you," he said when the noise did not let up. "Please," he asked, a note of desperation in his voice, motioning for everyone to sit down. That, at least, worked. "There we go. Good evening, San Francisco State University!"

More applause. Trish swore he winced. He sat on a stool in the middle of the stage, gestured and the lights went down. A single spotlight fell on him. Behind him, a screen lowered to the ground and a slideshow began.

"Technology," he started as the screen flashed images of attractive people on tablets and smartphones, "has an enormous transformative power. Instant communication has the power to topple governments and reshape societies at a rate of speed that our forefathers—Steve Jobs and Bill Gates—only dreamed of." The audience laughed at this joke. Longmire gave them a tight smile.

Trish studied him as he spoke. He'd obviously memorized his remarks—not surprising, given that the press had reported his IQ at 145—just above the threshold for a true genius. But when the audience responded in any way, he seemed to draw back, as if he didn't know what to do when he went off script. Excellent. That was exactly the sort of speaker who wouldn't know how to tap-dance out of a blatant donation request.

"And you are on the cusp of this technological revolution. You have that power at your fingertips, twenty-four hours a day, seven days a week." Longmire paused to take a drink from a water bottle and clear his throat. Trish had the distinct impression that he was forcing himself through this. *Interesting*, she thought.

"The problem then becomes one of inequality," Longmire went on. "How can you communicate with the rest of humanity if they don't have those things?" Images of tribal Africans, destitute southern Asians, aboriginals from Australia and—holy crap, had he actually found a picture of…Trish studied the photo hard before it clicked past. No, that hadn't been her reservation out in South Dakota, but it might have been the Rosebud lands.

Well. Yay for him acknowledging the state of the Native American reservations in a five-second picture, even if the montage did irritate her. All the people of color had been relegated to the poor section of the talk.

"We have a responsibility to use that power—that wealth," he went on, "for the betterment of our fellow humans on this planet…"

Longmire talked for another forty-five minutes, calling for the audience members to look beyond their own screens and be conscious consumers of technology. "Be engaged," he told them. "A rising tide lifts all boats. Solar-powered laptops can lift children out of poverty. Make sure the next Big Thing won't be lost to poverty and disease. It all starts with *you*." This time, when he smiled at the crowd, it was far more confident—and far more practiced. "Don't let me down."

The screen behind him shifted to the official Longmire Foundation photo with the Twitter handle and website. The crowd erupted into applause, giving him a six-minute standing ovation while Longmire half sat on his stool, drinking his water and looking like he'd rather be anywhere but here.

The emcee came back out on stage and thanked Longmire for his "absolutely brilliant" talk before she motioned to where the microphones had been set up in the aisles. "Mr. Longmire has agreed to take questions," Jennifer gushed.

Timing was everything. Trish didn't want to go first, but she didn't want to wait until the reporters started to pack up. She needed a lull that was just long enough for her to haul out her check and get to the microphone before anyone could stop her.

About ten students lined up in either aisle. Some questions were about how Longmire had started his company in his dorm room and how a regular student could come up with a billion-dollar idea.

"What's something that people need?" Longmire replied. "I wanted a way to take my digital photos with me. Adapting a simple idea that would make it easier to share photos with my parents—and make it easy for my parents to share those photos with other people—led me to adapting the SnAppShot app to every device, every platform available. It was ten years of hard work. Don't believe what the press says. There are no overnight successes in this business. See a need and fill it."

When he was replying, Trish noted, he had a different style. Maybe it was because he was really only talking to one person? But his words flowed more easily and he spoke with more conviction. The power in his words filled the auditorium. She could listen to that voice all night— he was *mesmerizing*.

This was a problem. Trish rubbed her hands on her jeans, trying to steady her nerves. Okay, so he spoke quite well off the cuff—which he demonstrated when a few people asked antagonistic questions.

Instead of acting trapped, Longmire's face would break into a sly smile—one completely different from the cautious movement of lips he'd used during his prepared remarks. Then he would dissect the question at an astonishing rate and completely undercut the argument, all without getting off the stool.

Ah, yes. This was his other reputation, the businessman who, much like his technological forefathers, would occasionally sue people for fun and profit. Nate Longmire had amassed the reputation of a man who never gave up and never surrendered in the courtroom. He'd completely bankrupted his former college friend, the one he'd started SnAppShot with.

Trish caught herself fidgeting with her earrings. Okay, yes—there was always the chance that her little stunt wouldn't go over well. But she was determined to give it a shot. The only people who lost were the ones who never tried.

Finally, there was only one person in line on her side and Longmire was listening intently to a question from the other aisle. Trish looked back and didn't see anyone else coming forward. This was it. She edged her check out from behind her seat and then stood in line, less than two feet away from the check. She could grab it and hoist it up in seconds. This would work. It had to.

The person in front of her asked some frivolous question about how Longmire felt about his status as a sex symbol. Even as Trish rolled her eyes, Longmire shot beet red. The question had unsettled him. Perfect.

"We have time for one more question," Jennifer announced after the nervous laughter had settled. "Yes? Step forward and say your name, please."

Trish bent over and grabbed her check. It was comically huge—a four-feet long by two-feet tall piece of cardboard. "Mr. Longmire," she said, holding the check in front of her like a shield. "My name is Trish Hunter and I'm the founder of One Child, One World, a charity that gets school supplies in the hands of underprivileged children on American Indian reservations."

Longmire leaned forward, his dark eyes fastened on hers. The world seemed to—well, it didn't fall away, not like it did in stories. But the hum of the audience and the bright lights seemed to fade into the background as Longmire focused all of his attention on her and said, "An admirable cause. Go on, Ms. Hunter. What is your question?"

Trish swallowed nervously. "I recently had the privilege of being named one of *Glamour*'s Top Ten College Women in honor of the work I'm doing." She paused to heft her check over her head. "The recognition came with a ten-thousand dollar reward, which I have pledged to One Child, One World in its entirety. You've spoken eloquently about how technology can change lives. Will you match this award and donate ten thousand dollars to help children get school supplies?"

The silence that crashed over the auditorium was deafening. All Trish could hear was the pounding of blood in her ears. She'd done it. She'd done *exactly* what she'd set out to do—cause a scene and hopefully trap one of the richest men in the world into parting with just a little of his hard-earned money.

"Thank you, Ms. Hunter," the emcee said sharply. "But Mr. Longmire has a process by which people can apply for—"

"Wait," Longmire cut her off. "It's true, the Longmire Foundation does have an application process. However," he said, his gaze never leaving Trish's face. Heat flushed her body. "One must admire a direct approach. Ms. Hunter, perhaps we can discuss your charity's needs after this event is over?"

Trish almost didn't hear the *Ooh*s that came from the rest of the crowd over the rush of blood in her ears. That wasn't a *no*. It wasn't a *yes*, either—it was a very good side step around giving a hard answer one way or the other. But it wasn't a *no* and that was all that mattered. She could still press her case and maybe, just maybe, get enough funding to buy every single kid on her reservation a backpack full of school supplies before school started in five months.

Plus, she'd get to see if Nate was as good-looking up

close as he was at a distance. Not that it mattered. Of course it didn't. "I would be honored," she said into the microphone and even she didn't miss the way her voice shook, just a little.

"Bring your check," he said with a grin that came real close to being wicked. "I'm not sure I've ever seen one that large before."

Laughter rolled through the auditorium as Longmire grinned at her. Behind his glasses, one eyebrow lifted in challenge and then he pointedly looked offstage. The message was clear. Would she meet him backstage?

The emcee was thanking Longmire for his time and everyone was applauding and the rest of the evening was clearly over. Trish managed to snag her small purse—a Coach knockoff—and fight against the rising tide of college kids who had not been invited backstage for a private meeting with the Boy Billionaire. With her small purse and her large check, Trish managed to get up the steps at the side of the stage and duck behind the curtains.

The emcee stood there, glaring at her. "That was some stunt you pulled," she said in a vicious whisper.

"Thanks!" Trish responded brightly. No doubt, Jennifer had had grand plans for her own post-interview "meeting" with Longmire and Trish had usurped that quite nicely.

"Ah, Ms. Hunter. Hello." Suddenly, Nate Longmire was standing before her. Trish was a good five-nine—taller in her boots—but she still had to lean her head up to meet his gaze. "Excellent," he went on, looking down at her as if he was thrilled to see her. "You have the large check. Jennifer, would you take our picture?"

His phone chimed. He looked at it, scowled briefly, and then called up his SnAppShot app. He handed his phone to the emcee, who forced a polite smile. "Hand it up here," Longmire said, taking half of the check in his hand. Then he put his arm around Trish's shoulders and whispered, "Smile."

Trish wasn't sure she pulled off that smile. His arm around her was warm and heavy and she swore to God that she felt his touch in places he wasn't touching.

She would not be attracted to him. She couldn't *afford* to be attracted to him. All she could do was forge ahead with her plan. Phase One—trap the Boy Billionaire—was complete. Now she had to move onto Phase Two—getting a donation out of him.

Forging ahead had absolutely nothing to do with the way his physical touch was sending shimmering waves of awareness through her body. *Nothing.*

Jennifer took two shots and then handed back the phone. Longmire's arm left her and Trish couldn't help it—she shivered at the loss of his warmth.

"Mr. Longmire," Jennifer began in a silky tone. "If you recall, I'd invited you out for a dinner after the program. We should get going."

There was a pause that could only be called awkward. Longmire didn't even move for three blinks of the eye— as if this statement had taken him quite by surprise and, despite his ferocious business skills and dizzying intellect, he had no possible answer for Jennifer.

Jennifer touched his arm. "Ready?" she said, batting her eyes.

Trish rolled hers—just as Longmire looked at her. *Oops.* Busted.

But instead of glaring at her, Longmire looked as if Trish was the answer to all his questions. That look should not do things to her. So, she forcibly decided, it didn't.

"Gosh—I do remember that, but I think I need to address Ms. Hunter's question first." He stepped away from Jennifer much like a crab avoiding a hungry seagull. Jennifer's hand hung in empty space for a moment before she lowered it back to her side. "Call my office," Longmire said, turning on his heel. "We'll try to set something up. Ms. Hunter? Are you coming?"

Trish clutched her check to her chest and hurried after Longmire, trying to match his long strides.

That definitely wasn't a *no*.

Now she just needed to get to a *yes*.

Nate settled into the Apollo Coffee shop. He liked coffee shops. They were usually busy enough that he didn't garner too much attention but quiet enough that he could think. He liked to think. It was a profitable, satisfying experience for him, thinking.

Right now he was thinking about the young woman who'd trucked a comically large check into the hired car and carried it into the coffee shop as if it were the most normal thing ever.

Trish Hunter. She was drinking a small black coffee—easily the cheapest thing on the extensive menu. She'd insisted on buying her own coffee, too. Had absolutely refused to let him plunk down the two dollars and change for hers.

That was something…different. He was intrigued, he had to admit.

The large check was wedged behind her chair, looking slightly worse for wear. "That's not the real check, is it?" he asked over the lip of his grande mocha.

"No. I got a regulation-sized check that went straight into the bank. But this makes for better photos, don't you think?" she replied easily, without that coy tone women had started using around him about the time he made his first million.

"Not a lot of people would have had the guts to try and trap me like that," he noted, watching her face closely. She was lovely—long dark hair that hung most of the way down her back, brown skin that graced high cheekbones. With her strong features and strong body—because there was no missing *that*—she looked like she could *be* Wonder Woman.

She didn't act like the kind of women who tried to trap him with their feminine wiles. Instead, she sat across from him, drinking cheap coffee and no doubt waiting to tell him why he should cut her another check.

For a second—the amount of time it took for her to look up at him through thick lashes—Nate almost panicked. He wasn't particularly good with women, as evidenced by that nagging feeling that he hadn't handled Jennifer's dinner invitation well and the fact that he had flat-out ignored that message from Diana—the third one this month.

Ever since things with Diana had fallen apart—and then really gone to hell—he'd kept things simple by simply not getting involved. Which meant that he was horribly out of practice. But there was no way he would let another woman take advantage of him. And that included Diana. Hence why he would just keep right on ignoring her messages.

Trish Hunter wasn't doing the things that normally made him nervous—treating him like he was a sex god she'd been secretly worshipping for years.

She grinned, a small curve of her lips over the edge of her cup. That grin did something to him—made him feel more sure of himself. Which sounded ridiculous but there it was. "Did it work? The trap, that is."

Nate smiled back. He was terrible about negotiations with members of the opposite sex. Money, however, was something he'd learned to negotiate. And the fact that this lovely young woman wasn't playing coy—wasn't acting like he'd gotten used to women acting around him—only made him more comfortable. Everything was out in the open. He could handle this kind of interaction. "That depends."

Her eyes widened slightly and a flash of surprise crossed her face. It made her look…innocent. Sweet, even. "Upon?"

"Tell me about your charity."

She exhaled in relief. It wasn't a big gesture, but he saw it nonetheless. He wondered what she'd thought he would ask. "Of course. One Child, One World is a registered 501(c) charity. We keep our overhead as low as possible." Nate sighed. He hated the boring part of charity work. It was, for lack of a better word, *boring.* "Approximately $0.93 of every dollar donated goes to school supplies…" her voice trailed off. "Not the right answer?"

He sat up a little straighter. She was paying attention to him. He'd be lying if he said it wasn't flattering. "Those statistics are all required as part of the grant application process," he replied, waving his hand. "The lawyers insisted. But that's not what I wanted to know."

She raised a strong eyebrow and leaned toward him. Yes, he had her full attention—and she had his. "You asked about my charity."

Oh, yeah—her words were nothing but challenge. This was not a woman telling him whatever he wanted to hear. This was a woman who would push back. Even though he had the money and she had a very cheap coffee, she'd still push back.

That made her even more interesting.

And as long as he kept thinking of it in terms of power and money—instead of noting how pretty she was and how she was looking at him and especially how he was no doubt looking at her—he'd be just fine.

"Tell me about why a young woman would start an organization to get school supplies into kids' hands. Tell me about…" *You.* But he didn't say that because that would cross the line of business and go into the personal. The moment he did that, he'd probably start flailing and knock the coffee into her lap. "Tell me about it."

"Ah." She took her time sipping her coffee. "Where did you grow up? Kansas City, right?"

"You've done your homework."

"Any good trap is a well-planned trap," she easily replied, a note of satisfaction in her voice.

He nodded his head in acknowledgment. "Yes, I grew up in Kansas City. Middle-class household. Father was an accountant, mother taught second grade." He left out the part about his brothers. "It was a very comfortable life." He hadn't realized how comfortable until he'd made his money—and started looking at how other people lived.

Trish smiled encouragingly. "And every August, you got a new backpack, new shoes, new school clothes and everything on that list teachers said you had to have, right?"

"Yes." He took a calculated risk. Just because she had black hair and skin the color of copper and was running a charity that helped American Indians on reservations didn't necessarily mean she was a Native American herself. But there was no such thing as coincidence. "I take it you didn't?"

Something in her face changed—her eyes seemed to harden. "My sixth-grade teacher gave me two pencils once. It was all she could afford." She dropped her gaze and began to fiddle with one of her earrings. "It was the best present I ever got."

Nate, being Nate, didn't have a smooth comeback to that. In fact, he didn't know what to say at all. His mom, Susan, had worked as a teacher, and she'd occasionally talked about a student who needed "a little extra help," as she put it. Then she'd fill a backpack with food and some basics and that was that. But that was before she'd had to stay home with Nate's brother Joe full-time.

"I'm sorry to hear that," he said quietly. Once, he hadn't

believed there was a world where a couple of #2 pencils were an amazing gift. But now he knew better.

Her gaze still on her coffee, she gave him a quick, tight smile. He needed to move the conversation forward. "So you're working to change that?"

"Yes. A new backpack full of everything a kid needs in a classroom." She shrugged and looked back at him. The hardness fell away. "I mean, that's the first goal. But it's an important first step."

He nodded thoughtfully. "You have bigger plans?"

Her eyes lit up. "Oh, of course! It's just the beginning."

"Tell me what you'd do."

"For so many kids, school is…it's an oasis in the middle of a desert. The schools need to open earlier, stay open later. They need to serve a bigger breakfast, a bigger lunch and everyone needs an afternoon snack. Too many kids aren't getting regular meals at home and it's so hard to study on an empty stomach." As she said this last point, she dropped her gaze again.

She was speaking from experience, he realized. Two pencils and nothing to eat at home.

"Indians on the rez love basketball and skateboarding," she went on. "Having better courts and parks on the school grounds could keep kids from joining gangs."

"You have gang problems?" He always associated gangs with inner-city drug wars or something.

She gave him a look that walked a fine line between "amused" and "condescending." "Some people have perverted our warrior culture into a gang mentality. We lose kids that way and we rarely get them back."

He thought over her wish list, such as it was. "I haven't heard anything about computers."

She paused, then gave him that tight smile again. "It's the ultimate goal, one that will require far more than ten or even twenty thousand dollars of funding. Most schools don't have the infrastructure to support an internet connection, much less cloud storage. I want kids to have basic supplies and full bellies before I get to that. You understand, don't you?"

He nodded. He'd toured some bad schools—mold growing on the walls, windows taped shut to keep the glass from falling out, ancient textbooks that smelled like rot. But what she was describing...

"What is it you want from me, then? Just ten grand?"

The moment he said it, he realized that maybe he shouldn't have phrased it quite like that. Especially not when Trish leaned back in her chair, one arm on the armrest, the other curled up under her chin—except for her index finger, which she'd extended over her lips as if they were in a library and she was shushing him. She met his gaze full-on, a hint of challenge lurking in her eyes. The air grew tight with tension.

God, she was beautiful and there was something else behind that gaze—an interest in more than just his bank account. He should ask her out. She wasn't intimidated by him and she wasn't throwing herself at him. She was here for the money and all her cards were up front, no hiding funding requests behind manipulative sexual desire. Hell. He didn't meet too many women who could just sit and have a conversation with him.

Except...dating was not his strong suit and he was pretty sure that asking a woman out right after she'd requested a donation would probably cross some ethical line.

Damn.

"Of course, One Child, One World would be delighted with any funding the Longmire Foundation saw fit to disperse," she said, sounding very much like someone who'd written a few grants in her time.

"How'd you get to be a Woman of the Year?"

"One of my professors nominated me," she told him. "I

didn't know she was doing it. One day, I'm trying to organize a bake sale to raise a hundred dollars to cover postage back to the rez and the next, I'm being flown to New York and given a *lot* of money." She blushed. "I mean, a lot of money for me. I'm sure ten grand isn't very much to you."

"I can remember when that much was a lot of money," he admitted. He winced. That was a totally jerky thing to say and he knew it.

He was about to apologize when she said, "Tell me about your charity," turning his question back on him.

He regarded her for a second. "Is that another way of asking why I'm giving money away for free?"

"You *did* go to all that trouble of earning it in the first place," she pointed out.

He shrugged. "Like I said, I had a comfortable childhood. We didn't always get everything we wanted—I didn't get a car for my sixteenth birthday or anything— but we were fine."

How he'd wanted a car. Brad, his older brother, had a half-rusted Jeep he'd bought with lawn-mowing money that he swore made it a breeze to get a date.

Back then, Nate had absolutely no prospect of a date. He was tall and gangly, with dorky glasses and awful skin. They were still trying to integrate Joe into a mainstream classroom at that point and Nate was mercilessly mocked by his peers. The only possible way he could have gotten a girl was if he'd had a sweet ride to pick her up in.

Alas. No car. No date.

"Anyway," he went on, shaking his head, "I made that first million and I felt like I'd made it. But a weird thing happened—that million spawned a second million, then a third. And then the buyout happened and now…" He gave her an apologetic smile. "Honestly, what the hell am I going to do with a billion dollars? Buy a country and rule as a despot?"

It wasn't as if this background was entirely new information—he'd given interviews explaining the rationale for his foundation—but those were formal things with scripted answers, preapproved by his assistant, Stanley.

Right now, sitting here in a coffee shop with Ms. Trish Hunter, it didn't feel like an interview. It felt like a conversation. An honest one.

Nate nodded toward her shirt. "I bought Superman #1—you know?"

A smile quirked at her lips. "I do know. Didn't you pay the highest recorded price for it?"

"I did. It was *wild*—I felt like I was jumping off a cliff, to pay five million for a comic book."

"Did you at least read it? Or did you lock it up?" The way she asked the question made it clear—she would have read it.

"I read it. Carefully." He waggled his eyebrows at her, as if he were saying something salacious. She laughed. It was as close to flirting as he got. "With tongs. In a temperature-controlled room."

Her eyes lit up. "Were you wearing one of those hazmat suits, too?"

"No. Just gloves." She giggled at the image and he laughed with her. It had been totally ridiculous. "But what else am I going to do with this much money besides buy comic books?"

"You donated a lot to mental-health research," she said. She was leaning forward slightly, her body language indicating that she was really listening.

"I have a…personal connection to that." When she waited for more, he added, "I keep my family private. It's the only way to stay sane in this industry."

Yes, he had set up an endowment into schizophrenia, depression and bipolar research. That was the public action. The private one had been setting up a trust fund for the care of Joe. Mom was able to stay home full-time with Joe now, and they had reliable home health aides to assist. Nate had tried to give his parents a million dollars or an all-expenses paid trip around the world, but it turned out that peace of mind about their youngest son was all they really wanted.

And after what had happened with Diana...

Nate's private life stayed private. Period.

"Ah, understood." She tilted her head. "That explains why there's no press on it. I wondered."

He stared at her. Yeah, he expected that she'd done her homework, but it was unusual to have someone admit to digging into his past—and then agree not to discuss it. As the shock of her blunt attitude wore off, he felt himself grinning at her even more. "Thanks. So, you know—I'm rich, I no longer run my own company—what am I going to do with the rest of my life? I set up a fund for my niece, bought my brother a house, took care of—well, I took care of the rest of my family, fended off a few lawsuits. That only left me with about a billion. Giving away the money seemed like something to do. The Longmire Foundation has given away fourteen million dollars and I haven't even made a dent yet."

That was the truth. He was making more in interest than he could give away. The simple truth was that her request for a matching grant of ten thousand dollars was the product of about five minutes for him, if that. He could add two or three zeroes to the end of the check and never even notice the money was gone.

"Is that what makes you happy?"

He looked at her funny. Happy? He was rich. He wasn't the same gangly nerd he'd been in high school. He was a ruthless businessman, a hugely successful one. He owned his own jet, for crying out loud.

But there was something in the way she asked it...

"I'm doing good. That's what counts."

"Of course." She opened her mouth, paused—and then angled her body toward his. Her gaze dropped again, but only for a second. She looked up at him through her lashes. Energy—attraction—seemed to arc between them as he stared at her.

Her eyes were a deep brown, like dark chocolate. Sweet, yes—but much more than that. There was innocence, but now it had an edge to it—an edge that held a hell of a lot of promise.

He leaned forward, eager to hear what she would say—and whether or not it would sound like legal boilerplate or if it would sound like something else.

He leaned right into his coffee and promptly spilled what was left of his grande mocha into her lap.

"Whoa!" she shouted, hopping to her feet. The dark stain spread down her leg.

"Oh, damn—I'm so sorry," he mumbled. What had he been thinking? Of course she wasn't going to say something along the lines of "Maybe we should discuss this over dinner." He grabbed some napkins and thrust them at her. "Here."

This was terrible. He'd been doing just fine when it'd been a business negotiation, but the moment he hoped it'd go past that—it blew up in his face.

"I'm so sorry," he repeated. "I'll pay for the cleaning bill."

She laughed. And after she'd checked her seat for coffee, she sat down, spread a napkin over her lap, and grinned at him. "Don't worry about it."

"But your clothes…" Even now, he could see the droplets of coffee on her shirt.

"I'm used to spills and stains. Don't worry about it."

He wasn't sure if he believed her, but then he met her gaze. It was full of humor, yes—but he didn't get the sense that she was laughing at him. Just the situation. Clumsy billionaire knocks coffee into her lap.

He had to get out of here before he did even worse damage to her clothes or his pride. "Listen, why don't you come by my office in two weeks? I'll have my assistant start the paperwork and we can settle the terms then." He fished out his card, which just said, "Longmire Foundation," with the address and email. "And please—bring the dry-cleaning bill. It hurts me to think that I might have ruined your shirt."

A second too late, he realized he was staring at her chest. The jacket had fallen open a little more. It was a very nice chest.

God, what was he doing? Trying to make this worse? He shook some sense—he hoped—back into his head and handed over the card. "Say, Friday at two?"

"I have to work." She took the card and studied it. "This is in the Filmore area."

"Yes. I keep an office close to where I live." She was still looking at the card. "Is that a problem?"

"No, it's fine. I just thought you'd be down in the Mission or in SOMA. Close to where all the other tech billionaires hang out."

He waved his hand. "I like to walk to the office when it's nice out." She gaped at him, as if she couldn't believe a billionaire would stoop to walking on his own two feet instead of being carried on a gold-plated litter by trained elephants. "Truth be told, we're not some sort of secret billionaire club. And I don't really have much interest in the constant one-upmanship that happens when you get us all together. I like peace and quiet and a nice view. I like to be a little bit not what people expect."

That got her attention. She looked up at him, her dark eyes wide and...encouraging?

If she could still look at him after he dumped his drink all over her, then maybe…

She went back to studying the card. "I won't be able to get there until five. Is that too late?"

"Yeah, that's fine. I'll make sure Stanley knows you're coming."

"Stanley?"

"My assistant." Actually, Stanley was more than that—he picked out Nate's clothes and made sure Nate projected the right amount of geek-cred cool. If only Stanley had been here tonight, no one would have gotten a damp lap.

He'd have Stanley start the due diligence on her charity to make sure her numbers were correct.

She grinned up at him again, as if she wasn't sure how to process an assistant named Stanley. "I look forward to our meeting." She stood, crumpling up the napkins and stuffing them into her empty cup. Then she extended her hand. "Mr. Longmire, it has been an honor. Thank you so much for considering my proposal."

"It's a worthy cause." He took her hand in his and tried to shake it, but the feeling of her slender fingers warming his momentarily froze his brain. He wanted to say something suave and sophisticated that let her know he was interested in more than her charity.

He had nothing.

Maybe their next meeting would go more smoothly—in his office, Stanley would be ready to swoop in and save Nate from himself as needed. "And again—sorry about the coffee."

She waved him off and retrieved her large check from behind the chair. Thankfully, it didn't seem to be too splattered. "I'll see you on Friday in two weeks."

"I'm looking forward to it." That got him a nice smile, warm and friendly and comforting—like she realized exactly how socially awkward he really was and was rewarding him for doing a decent job.

Nate watched her figure retreat from the coffee shop and disappear into the foggy darkness, the check glowing white. Trish Hunter. Yes, Stanley would have to do some due diligence on her charity. And on the woman herself. Nate wanted to know more about her—a lot more.

He sent for a car to take him home and was picking up the coffee cups—his mother had always taught him to pick up after himself and being a self-made billionaire hadn't changed that—when his phone rang. Not the chime that went with a message, but the ring of someone actually calling him.

His mother. She was pretty much the only person who called him, anyway. She was too old to learn to text, she said. That was her story and she was sticking to it.

"Hey, Mom," he said, heading out to the sidewalk.

"Nate? Oh, honey." She was crying. Nate froze halfway out the door. Instantly, all thoughts of Trish Hunter and large checks and coffee were pushed from his mind.

"Mom? What's wrong?"

"Nate—oh, God. There's been an accident."

"Dad?" Panic clawed at him. His parents were only in their fifties. He didn't want to lose either one just yet.

"He's fine. Oh, Nate…we need you to come home. It's Brad and Elena…"

"Are they okay?" But even as he said it, he knew the answer was no. His mother was crying. Something horrible had happened to his older brother and his sister-in-law. "What about Jane?" When his mom didn't answer right away, Nate nearly threw up. "Mom—is Jane okay?"

"The baby is fine. We were watching her so they could go out… Come home, Nate. Come home *now*."

Dear God in heaven. "I'm on my way, Mom. I'll be there as soon as I can." He hung up and called Stanley. This was one of the benefits of being a billionaire. He didn't have to deal with emergency flights. He had an assistant—and a private jet.

"Stanley, get the plane ready. I need to go to Kansas City. Right now."

Two

Trish had spent a good deal of time on this outfit. Wearing the Wonder Woman shirt again would be too obvious, even though it had washed clean. Trish had decided to go a little more formal for this meeting. She had on a coral skirt that came to midcalf. She'd paired it with a white shirt that was as crisp as she could get it in a public Laundromat and a denim jacket from Diesel—another major score from the thrift stores. Her only pair of cowboy boots were on her feet. Once they'd been black, but now they were a faded gray. Which was trendy enough, so she figured she was okay.

She was wearing the one good piece of turquoise she had, a teardrop-shaped pendant that hung on a thin silver chain. She'd twisted her hair up into a professional looking knot and had put in a pair of silver hoops that looked more expensive than they really were.

This was her being a business-professional Lakota woman. This was not her dressing to impress a certain billionaire. Not much, anyway.

She didn't have a cleaning bill to give him and she had the distinctive feeling that he wasn't going to be happy about that. What could she do? Tell him she needed $1.25 in quarters for the Laundromat?

The skirt had necessitated the bus, however. She hadn't wanted it to get tangled up in her bike spokes. So, at 5:08—

after almost an hour and a half—she finally arrived at his address in the Filmore district.

The Longmire Foundation was on the fourth floor of an austere-looking office building. On the ride up, Trish swallowed nervously. Yes, the conversation with Nate at the coffee shop had been pleasant and encouraging—but who knew what might have changed in the past two weeks? Because of how the event had played out in the press, she was worried that he might have changed his mind. The news reports had caught the look he'd given her when he'd asked her to meet him backstage and rumors about something else happening backstage had already started.

Trish had fielded a few phone calls, which was good. Sort of. Yes, any attention she could draw to One Child was good attention—but the quotes reporters had been looking for were much more along the lines of whether or not a romance had sparked.

Which it hadn't. Really.

So Nate Longmire was tall, built and twice as handsome in person as he was in photographs. So there'd been something between them—something that she hadn't been able to stop thinking about since the moment she'd walked out of that coffee shop. It'd almost been like…like she'd belonged there, with him. For just a little bit, he hadn't been some unreachable Boy Billionaire and she hadn't been a dirt-poor American Indian. He'd just been a man and she'd just been a woman and that was—well, it was good. With the potential to be even better.

And that potential? That's what she'd been dreaming about almost every single night for the past two weeks.

Well. They were just dreams. And she needed to stick with reality.

And the reality of the situation was that Nate was not her type. She didn't have a type, but whatever it might be, a Boy Billionaire clearly wasn't it. She would probably never have a total of five million dollars in her entire life—and he was the kind of guy who spent that on a comic book.

At least the Wonder Woman shirt had done its job, she figured. Now, in her fancy clothes, it was time to do hers.

She'd done her best to avoid answering any questions about her supposed involvement with Nate Longmire by throwing out every single stat she could about poverty on Indian reservations and how even a five-dollar donation could make a difference. In the end, unable to get a juicy quote out of her, the press had left her alone.

She'd noticed that, in any report, whether online or on television, Nate Longmire had always been "unavailable for comment." She didn't know if that was a good thing or not.

Trish found the right door—suite 412, *The Longmire Foundation* written in black letters on the glass—and tried the doorknob, but it was locked. A growing sense of dread filled her as she knocked.

A minute passed. Trish didn't know if she should knock again or…what? She had no other options. Nate said he'd be here—that Stanley would be here. He hadn't forgotten, had he?

She knocked again.

This time, a man shouted, "Jeez, I'm coming. I'm coming."

The door was unlocked and thrown open. Instead of Nate Longmire's well-dressed form, a man in a white tank top, oversize corduroy pants held up by bright red suspenders and more tattoos than God glared down at her. "What?"

"Um, hello," Trish said, trying not to be nervous. This guy had spacers in his ears. She could see right through them. She swallowed. "I have an appointment with Mr. Longmire—"

"What are you doing here?" the man all but growled at her.

"I'm sorry?"

The man looked put out. "You're supposed to be at his house for the interview. Didn't they tell you that?"

They? They *who*? "No?"

Mr. Tattoos rolled his eyes to the sky and sighed. "You're in the wrong place. You need to be at 2601 Pacific Street." He looked at her dubiously. "2601 Pacific Street," he repeated in a slower, louder voice, as if she'd suddenly gone deaf. When Trish just stared at him, he pointed again and said, "That way. Okay?"

"Yes, all right." She stood there for a minute, too shocked to do much but not look through the holes in his ears. "Thank you."

"Yeah, good luck—you're gonna need it," he called after her, then she heard the door shut and lock behind her.

Great. Trish was going to be way late. Panic fluttered through her stomach. Was this a sign—Nate had reviewed her case and decided that her charity didn't meet his requirements? Why on earth was she supposed to go to his house—especially if he was going to turn her down? This wasn't about to get weird, was it?

She did the only thing she could do—she started to walk. She loved walking through San Francisco, looking at all the Victorian houses and wondering what it would be like to live in one. To have a view of the bay or the Golden Gate Bridge. To not have to worry about making rent and having enough left over.

Her mother, Pat, had loved the music from the Summer of Love. When she was with a real jerk of a boyfriend—which was often enough—Pat would sometimes get nostalgic and talk about one day coming out to San Francisco to find Trish's father. That was how Trish found out that her father had come to this city when he'd abandoned his family.

Trish did what she always did when she walked the

streets—she looked in the faces of each person she passed by, hoping to recognize a little part of herself. Maybe her father had gotten remarried and had more kids. Maybe Trish would find a half sister walking around. Or maybe the woman her father had settled down with would recognize her husband's face in Trish's and ask if they were related.

Trish had lived here for five years. This on-the-street recognition hadn't happened, not once. But she kept looking.

She walked to Pacific Street and turned. This was such a beautiful place, right across from the park. Nothing like the tiny garret apartment in Ingleside she rented for the subsidized sum of $350 a month.

She found the right house—she hoped. It was a sweeping three-story Victorian home, the exterior painted a soft shade of blue with bright white paint outlining the scrollwork and columns. The curtains on the ground-level windows were closed and a painted garage door was shut. Next to that was a wide, sweeping set of steps that led up to the perfect porch for a summer afternoon, complete with swing.

It was simply lovely. The small part of her brain that wasn't nervous about this whole "interview at his house" thing was doing a little happy dance—she would finally get to see the inside of one of these homes.

But that excitement was buried pretty danged deep. To get inside the home, she had to get through the gate at the bottom of the stairs—and it didn't budge. How was she supposed to be *at* the house if she couldn't even get to the door? Then she saw a buzzer off to the right. She pressed it and waited.

Even standing here felt like she was interloping again. This wasn't right. Nate had been very clear—she was to meet him at the office. Trish had no idea which "they" should have told her about the change, but what could she do? She needed the donation, desperately.

So she rang the bell, again, and waited. Again. She caught herself twisting her earring and forced her hands back by her sides. This was not about to go sideways on her. This was fine. She was a professional. She could handle whatever was on the other side of that door with grace and charm.

Up on the porch, the door opened and a short, stocky woman in a gray dress and a white apron stood before her. "Hello?"

"Hi," Trish said, trying her best to smile warmly. "I have an appointment with Mr. Longmire and—"

"*Ay mia*—you're late," the woman said—but unlike Mr. Tattoo, she looked happy to see Trish. "Come in, come in." A buzzer sounded and the gate swung free. Trish climbed the stairs, schooling her features into a professional smile—warm, welcoming, not at all worried about the lack of communication about any changes to the plan.

"Hello," she said when she was face-to-face with the woman. "I'm Trish Hunter and—"

The woman latched onto Trish's arm and all but hauled her inside. The door shut with a resounding thud behind her.

"Who is it, Rosita?" Trish recognized Nate's voice as the one calling down the stairs.

"The girl," Rosita called back.

"Send her up."

It was only then, with Rosita the maid shooing her up the stairs so fast that she could barely take in the beautiful details of the entry room, that Trish heard it—the plaintive wail of a deeply unhappy baby.

It was pretty safe to say that Trish had absolutely no idea what was going on. But up the stairs she went, bracing herself for what baby-related carnage awaited her.

She was not wrong about that.

Nate Longmire—the same Boy Billionaire who had given an impassioned talk on social responsibility, the same Nate Longmire who had insisted on paying her dry-cleaning bill, the very same Nate Longmire that had looked positively sinful in his hipster glasses and purple tie—stood in front of one of those portable playpens that Trish had coveted for years. Nate was in a pair of jeans and a white T-shirt. That part wasn't surprising.

What was surprising was that Nate was trying to hold a screaming baby. The child was in nothing but a diaper and, unless Trish missed her guess, the diaper was on backwards.

"What on earth?" Trish demanded.

Nate spun at the sound of the exclamation from behind him just as Jane squirmed in his arms. Oh, hell—why were babies so damned hard to hold onto?

"Uh..." he managed to get out as he got his other arm under Jane's bottom and kept her from tumbling. The little girl screamed even louder. Nate would have thought that it was physically impossible for her to find more volume from her tiny little body, but she had.

"Oh, for Pete's sake," the woman said. The next thing he knew, Jane had been lifted out of his arms by a beautiful woman with striking dark eyes and—

Oh, God. "Trish!"

"Yes, hello," she said, slinging the baby onto her hip with a practiced air. "Where are the diapers?"

"Why—what—I mean—you're here?"

Trish paused in her search for diapers and gave him a look. It was a look that he deserved. Never in his entire life had he felt more like an idiot. "Yes. We had an appointment."

He started. "Your appointment?"

"Yes," she said, as she turned a small circle, surveying the complete and total destruction of the room that, until seven days ago, had been a sitting room and now was supposed to be a nursery. Even Nate knew that it wasn't a nursery, not yet. It was a hellhole. He couldn't tell if she was finding what she was looking for or not.

His mind tried to work, but that was like trying to open a bank vault where all the tumblers had rusted shut. He was *so* tired but Trish was here. He'd never been so happy to see a woman in his entire life. "You're here about the nanny position?"

That got him another look—but there was more pity in her eyes this time. "Mr. Longmire," she said in an utterly calm voice. She snagged a blanket and, with the screaming baby still on her hip, managed to smoothly lay the cloth out on the floor. "We had an appointment in your office at five today to discuss a matching grant to my charity, One Child, One World."

Oh, hell. "You're...not here about the nanny position?"

Trish located a diaper and then fell to her knees in an entirely graceful way. She carefully laid Jane out on the blanket. "Oh, dear, yes," she soothed in a soft voice that Nate had to strain to hear over the screaming. "You're so cold, sweetie! And wet, too? Oh, yes, it's so hard to be a baby, isn't it?" Trish changed the diaper and then looked up at him. "Does she have any clothes?"

"Why are you so calm?" he demanded.

"This is not difficult, Mr. Longmire. Does she have any clothes?"

Nate turned and dug into one of the suitcases Stanley had loaded onto his private plane. "Like a dress or something?"

"Like jammies, Mr. Longmire. Oh, I know," she said in that soothing voice again. "I know. I think he's trying his best, but he doesn't know how to speak baby, does he?"

For a blissful second, Jane stopped screaming and instead only made a little burbling noise, as if she really were talking to Trish.

Then the screaming started right back up with renewed vigor.

Nate grabbed something that looked like it could be jammies. Orange terry cloth with pink butterflies and green flowers, it had long sleeves and footies attached to the legs. "This?"

"That's perfect," Trish said in that soothing tone again. Nate handed over the clothes and watched, stunned, as Trish got the wriggling arms and kicking legs into the fabric.

"How do you do that? I couldn't get her into anything. And I couldn't get her to stop screaming."

"I noticed." Trish looked up at him and smiled. "How are you feeding her?"

"Um, my mom sent some formula. Down in the kitchen."

Trish rubbed Jane's little tummy. Then, like it was just that easy, she folded the blanket around Jane and tucked in the ends and suddenly, Nate was looking at a baby burrito.

"One second, baby." Then, to Nate, she said, "Don't pick her up—but watch her while I wash my hands, okay?"

"Okay?" What choice did he have? The baby was still crying but, miraculously, her volume had pitched down for the first time since Nate had seen her.

"Bathroom?" Trish asked.

"Through that door." As he stared at Jane, he tried to think. For a man who had done plenty of thinking while pulling all-nighters, he was stunned at how much his brain felt like the sludge at the bottom of a grease trap.

Trish Hunter. How could he forget her? Not even a funeral or a solid two weeks of sleep deprivation could erase the memory of her talking with him in a coffee shop. She'd been smart and beautiful and he'd—he'd liked her. He'd gotten the distinctive feeling that she'd been interested in him—not just his money.

Crap. He must have forgotten about their appointment entirely when his world fell apart. Which—yes, now he remembered—had occurred moments after his conversation with Trish in the coffee shop.

The woman he'd felt a connection with was the same woman who had just walked into his house and changed his niece's diaper.

Wait.

A woman he'd felt a connection with had just changed his niece's diaper. And gotten her dressed. And wrapped her into a burrito. And, if the indications were to be believed, was about to go down and fix a bottle of formula.

He'd been expecting a candidate for the position of nanny.

Maybe she had arrived.

Trish came out, looking just as elegant as she had before. "There now," she said in that soft voice as she scooped Jane up and cuddled the baby against her chest. "I bet you're hungry and I bet you're sleepy. Let's get some milk, okay?" Jane made a little mewing sound that came close to an agreement.

Trish looked at Nate, who was staring. "Kitchen?"

"This way."

Nate felt like he needed to be doing something better here—but he was at a loss. All he could do was lead the way down stairs and into the back of the house, where Rosita was looking like the last rat on the ship. When his maid saw Trish cuddling the slightly quieter baby, her face lit up. "Oh, miss—we're so glad you've come."

Trish managed a smile, but Nate saw it wasn't a natural thing. "Any clean bottles and nipples?"

Rosita produced the supplies, babbling on in her faint accent the whole time. "I tried, miss, but I never much cared for children." She got out the tub of formula and a gallon of milk and started to mix it.

"Wait—stop." Trish's voice was one of horror. Then she looked at Nate and then around the room again, just like she had in the nursery. When she settled upon the breakfast bar with the stools, she said, "Mr. Longmire—sit."

He sat.

"Hold out your arms like this." She slid Jane down into a cradled position. Nate did as she asked. "Good. Now. Don't drop the baby." Trish set Jane into his arms and then ran her hands over him, pushing his arms tighter here, looser there. Even in his exhausted state, he didn't miss the way her touch lingered on his skin.

He looked up at her. Her face was only inches away from his. If possible, she was even prettier today than she'd been in the coffee shop.

"I'm so glad you're here," he said. It came out quiet and serious.

She paused and met his gaze, her hands still on his bare skin. Heat flashed between them, that attraction he'd felt before.

She didn't say anything, though. She just kept arranging his body until—for the first time—Nate felt like he had a good grasp on his niece.

Although he still didn't have a good grasp on the situation. Well, one thing at a time. Baby first. Attraction second.

"All right," Trish said, sounding very much like a general about to engage in battle. "Dump that out, please. Do you have any other clean bottles?"

"Miss?" Rosita said, hesitantly.

"No milk, not yet. The formula's supposed to be mixed with water."

"Oh," Rosita and Nate said at the same time. Nate went on, "My mom just said she needed her milk every three hours and I thought…damn. I mean dang," he corrected, looking down at Jane.

"I am so sorry, Señor Nate," Rosita said in a low voice. "I…"

"Don't worry about it, Rosita. We both missed it. No harm done." He glanced back at Trish. "Right?"

"Probably not," Trish replied as she fixed a fresh bottle. "Is there somewhere we can go sit? I have a few questions."

"Yeah." She took the baby out of his arms and waited for him to lead the way.

Nate couldn't go back up to the disaster zone that was supposed to be the nursery. That was no image to present to anyone, but especially a lovely young woman who had a way with a baby and hadn't run screaming at the sight of Nate at his worst.

"Rosita, if you could try and make some sense of the nursery while Ms. Hunter and I talk?"

"Yes," Rosita said, sounding relieved to be off the hook. She scurried out of the kitchen faster than Nate had ever seen her move in the three years she'd worked for him.

Nate led Trish to his front parlor. He liked this old house, these old rooms. He kept his technology in a separate room so that this room, where he received visitors, had a timeless feel to it. The front parlor was an excellent room within which to think. No blinking lights or chiming tones to distract him—or disturb an upset infant. "Where do you want to sit?"

"This will be fine." She settled herself in his favorite chair, the plush leather wingback with a matching footstool. She propped her arm on the armrest and got Jane to take the bottle on the second try. Nate watched in surprise. He had hardly been able to get Jane to drink anything.

Of course, if they'd been making it wrong…

"So," she said when he perched on the nearby sofa. "Tell me about it."

Nate didn't like to talk about his family. He liked to keep that part of himself—his past, their present—private. It was better that way for everyone. But he was desperate here. "This doesn't leave this room."

She lifted her eyebrows, but that was the only sign that his statement surprised her. "Agreed."

"I didn't mean to forget our appointment."

"It's pretty obvious that something came up. Didn't it, sweetie?" she cooed at Jane, who was making happy little slurping noises. Nate was thrilled to see her little eyelids already drifting shut.

"I haven't slept more than two hours at a shot in the last two weeks. I don't…I told my parents I couldn't do this. I don't know anything about babies."

"Agreed," Trish repeated with a smile. Nate became aware of a light humming that sounded like…a lullaby?

He took a deep breath. He'd only told two other people about what had happened—Stanley and Rosita. "My brother, my perfect older brother, and his wife left Jane— that's the baby—with my parents to go out to dinner."

The humming stopped and Trish got very still. "And?"

He knew how bad it was to look weak—he'd almost lost his company back at the beginning because he'd been trying to be a nice guy and Diana didn't play by those rules. He'd learned never to show weakness, especially not in the business world.

But the horror of the past two weeks was almost too much for him. He dropped his head into his hands. "And they didn't make it back. A semi lost control, flipped over. They…" The words clogged up in his throat. "They didn't suffer."

"Oh my God, Nate—I'm so sorry." He looked at her and was surprised to see tears gathering in her eyes. "That's— oh, that's just horrible."

"I mean, Brad—that was my brother—you know, it

was hard to grow up in his shadow. He was good-looking and he was the quarterback and he got all the girls. He took—" Nate bit down on the words. He'd made his peace with Brad. Mostly. He'd done his best to put aside the betrayal for the sake of their mother. "We'd...we'd started to become friends, you know? It wasn't a competition anymore because he could never beat me in money and I could never beat him in looks and we were finally even. *Finally.*"

In the end, Brad had done him a favor, really. At least, that's how Nate *had* to look at, for his sanity's sake.

There was a somewhat stunned silence as Trish stared at him, punctuated only by the noises of Jane eating. "For what it's worth," she said in a quiet voice, deeper than the one she used on the baby, "you are an incredibly attractive man."

There it was again—that challenge, that something else that seemed to draw the air between them tighter than a bowstring. For a second, he was too stunned to say anything. He didn't feel attractive right now—just as he hadn't felt attractive when he'd been named one of Silicon Valley's Top Ten Bachelors.

But Trish—beautiful and intelligent and obviously much more knowledgeable about babies than he'd ever be—thought he was attractive. *Incredibly* attractive.

He realized he was probably blushing. "Sorry," he said, trying to keep control of himself. "I don't know why I told you that about my brother. I..."

"You've had a long couple of weeks. When did the accident happen?"

"I got the call as I was leaving the coffee shop. I guess that's why I didn't remember you were coming. I'm sorry about that, too."

"Nate," she said in a kind voice and Nate's mind went back to the way she'd touched him in the kitchen. If only he could think straight… "It's all right. I understand. Life happens."

"Yeah, okay." He could do with a little less life happening right now, frankly.

"So your brother and sister had a baby girl?"

"Jane. Yes."

"Jane," Trish said, the name coming off her tongue like a sigh. "Hello, Jane." But then she looked back at Nate. "If you don't mind me asking, why do *you* have Jane? What about your parents?"

Nate dropped his head back into his hands. It was still so hard to talk about. There wasn't the same stigma now, but back when he'd been a kid… "They couldn't take her."

"Not even for a week or so? No offense, but you don't have a baby's room up there. You have a death trap."

"I—" He swallowed. "I have another brother."

There was that stillness again. She was 100 percent focused on him.

"He's severely mentally ill."

"You say that like it's a bad thing."

"It's not. Not anymore. But there were…problems. He was institutionalized for a while until we could get the meds straightened out." He shrugged. "He's my brother and I love him. He loved Brad, too. Brad was his buddy. They'd go out and throw the football around…" His throat seemed to close up on him and he had to swallow a couple of times to get things to work again.

Trish looked at him like she wanted to comfort him. But she said, "No one knows about your brother?"

"In the past, other people have tried to use that against me. Against my family. And I will not stand for it." The last part came out meaner than he meant it to. She wasn't a threat. She wasn't Diana.

"You give to mental illness research."

"Because of Joe, yeah." He sighed. "He needs his routine. My mom takes care of him and I pay for home health workers. But the last few weeks, my parents have been so upset about Brad and Elena… Besides," he added, feeling the weight of the words, "I'm her legal guardian."

"I see," she replied. "Oh, that's a good girl, Jane. Here." She handed Nate the bottle and then casually moved the baby to her shoulder and began patting Jane's back. "So you're trying to hire a nanny?"

"Yeah. You want the job?"

Trish paused in midpat, and then laughed a little too forcefully. "That's not why I'm here."

He wasn't about to take *no* as an answer. So he didn't always know what to do around members of the opposite sex. He knew how to negotiate a business deal. He needed a nanny. She needed money.

"What do you mean? You obviously know what you're doing." The more he thought about it, the better he liked this idea. He'd already sort of interviewed her, after all. He liked her. Okay, maybe that wasn't a good enough reason to offer her a job changing diapers and burping a baby, but he was comfortable with her and she knew what she was doing and *that* counted for something.

She sighed. "Of course I do. My mom had nine kids with…four different men. Then she married my current stepfather, who had four kids of his own with two other women. I'm the oldest."

Nate tried to process that information. "Your mom had ten kids?"

"Not that she took care of them," Trish replied and for the first time, he heard a distinctive note of bitterness in her voice.

"You?"

Her smile was tight. "Me."

"Perfect."

"Excuse me?"

"Look, I need a nanny. More than that, I need *you*. I've had three people come to the door and no one's made it past five minutes, whereas you've gotten Jane to calm down and stop screaming. I swear this is the first time in two weeks I've been able to hear myself think."

And all of that had nothing to do with the way Trish had touched him, so he was still acting aboveboard here.

"Mr. Longmire," she said in a deeply regretful tone, "I can't. I'm due to graduate with my master's degree in a month and a half. I need to finish my studies and—"

"You can study here. When she sleeps."

Trish's eyes flashed in defiance, which made him smile. "I work two jobs," she went on, in a stronger voice. "I do research for the professor who nominated me for the *Glamour* award and I answer phones in the department."

This was much better. She was negotiating. And God knew that, despite the fact that he was so tired he was on the verge of seeing two Trishes cuddling two babies, he could negotiate a business deal. "For, what? Ten dollars an hour?"

Her back stiffened. "Twelve-fifty, if you must know, but that's not the point."

He felt himself grinning. This was what he'd liked in the coffee shop. She wasn't afraid to push back. She wasn't afraid to challenge him. "What is the point?"

"I have a plan. I have school obligations and employment obligations and charitable obligations that I *will* meet. I have to start organizing the back-to-school drive now. I can't drop everything just to nanny your niece. You'll find a perfectly qualified nanny, I'm sure."

"I already have."

"*No*, Mr. Longmire."

He did some quick calculations in his head. He had to keep her here with him. He needed her in a way he'd never needed any other woman. Everyone had a breaking point. Where was hers?

"I will personally call your professor and explain that you've been selected for a unique opportunity."

Her eyes flew wide in disbelief. "You wouldn't."

"Obviously you'll finish your degree, but you'll need to stay here during the month. Sleep here."

"Excuse me?" She looked indignant. The baby, who had actually stopped crying and was possibly asleep, startled and began to make mewing noises.

"I'll pay you five thousand dollars for one month."

Whatever biting rejection she'd been about to say died in a gurgling noise in the back of her throat. "What?"

"One month. I can probably find another nanny in that amount of time, but I need you now."

"Mr. Longmire—"

"Nate."

"*Mister* Longmire," she went on with whispered emphasis. The baby mewed again. Without appearing to think about it, Trish stood and began rocking from side to side.

Yeah, he was looking at his nanny. "One month. A temporary nanny position."

"I'll lose my lease. I'm—I can't afford much. My landlord wants me out so she can triple the rent."

"Ten thousand."

All the blood drained out of her face, but she didn't answer.

"Come on, Ms. Hunter. Ten grand could get you set up in a nice apartment. For one month of teaching me how to care for my niece and helping me find a more permanent nanny. I'd hazard a guess that you'd be moving out of that apartment after graduation, anyway. This can be the nanny plan. Just a slight change to your original plan."

Her mouth opened. "A *slight* change?"

Which was not a *no*, but also wasn't an agreement to

his terms. Where was her breaking point? Then it hit him. The charity.

"Twenty thousand," he said, impulsively doubling the salary. *Let's see her say no to that*, he thought. "In addition to that salary, I'm prepared to make a donation to the One Child, One...whatever it was. One hundred thousand dollars."

Trish collapsed back into the seat, which jostled the baby. She quickly stood again, but instead of rocking from side to side, she turned and walked to the window. "You wouldn't do that."

"I can and I will." She didn't reply. He realized she wasn't necessarily playing hardball with him, but what the hell did a couple hundred grand mean to him? Nothing. He'd never even miss it, but he might change her life. "Fine. Two-fifty. My final offer."

"Two...fifty?" She sounded like she was being strangled.

"Two hundred and fifty thousand dollars to your very worthy charity, to be paid half now, half at the end of the month, provided you stay here, handle the night feedings and whatever else has Jane up every two hours, and teach me how to do some of the basics."

"And...hire a permanent replacement?"

He had her then. She couldn't say no to that kind of cash and they both knew it. "That's the plan, yes."

She didn't reply and he let the silence stretch. Final offers and all that.

He watched her as she thought it over. She was gently rocking from side to side and he could see the top of Jane's fuzzy little head over Trish's shoulder. It looked...something in his chest clenched. It was probably just the sleep deprivation but, Trish standing at the window, soothing the baby—it looked *right*, somehow.

Was he really doing this—convincing this beautiful

woman to stay here, with him? To sleep under the same roof with him? What the hell? He'd wanted to ask her out, not move her in. Still, if she were living in his house...

Stay, he thought. *Stay here. With me.*

"This..." She took an exceptionally deep breath. "This *generous* donation—it's not contingent upon anything else?"

"Such as?"

"I can't sleep with you."

He let out a bark of a laugh, which caused her to half turn and *shush* him. "Do I look that bad?"

"I didn't mean to offend." Her gaze flicked over him again and he simultaneously remembered the sad state of his shirt and that earlier she'd decreed he was attractive. *Incredibly* attractive. He sat up a little straighter. "It's just that...I don't sleep with anyone."

That seems a crying shame.

The words waltzed right up to the tip of his tongue, but even in his sleep-deprived state, he knew better than to say them out loud.

She looked down at Jane's head. "I've raised *so* many babies already. Whatever money doesn't go to the charity directly goes to support my siblings. My youngest sister is nine. And I..." She sighed and looked out the window. The fog was starting to roll in. "I want her to have more than two pencils."

She turned back to him, determination blazing in her eyes. "It's not that I don't appreciate your generous offer, but there's more that I can do than change diapers and make bottles. I know exactly what sacrifices it takes to raise a child and I..." She glanced down at the baby in her arms and sighed heavily. "I'm not ready to make those sacrifices again. Not just yet."

"One month. That's all I need, Trish. And it's not contingent upon you sleeping with me." She raised her eyebrow at him, as if she doubted his resolve. "I give you my word of honor. Sex is not a part of the plan." He wasn't terribly good at seduction, anyway.

However, there was nothing in their bargain that ruled out him asking for a date after the month was up.

She got a weird look on her face, like she was trying not to smile and not quite making it.

"I just—look," he stammered, trying to recover. "I just need...you. You're perfect."

From this angle—the warming light coming through the window, her face half-turned to him—he couldn't tell if she was blushing or not. But she dropped her gaze and said, "One month. No sex."

"Twenty grand payment for you and two hundred fifty thousand dollars to your charity. Agreed."

She exhaled. "I want it in writing."

"Done. By tomorrow. But..."

"But what?"

"Will you stay tonight?" The words felt foreign on his tongue. He didn't ask women to stay over, not since the thing with Diana had wound up in court.

Her mouth—her deep pink lips—opened and shut before they opened again. "I have to get my things."

A spike of panic hammered into Nate's head. "What if she wakes up? While you're gone?"

"I won't be long. Here. Sit in the chair." She motioned toward the seat she'd just left. "I'll put her on your chest and she'll probably sleep for a few hours. Maybe you can get some sleep, too." She gave him a sly grin. "You look like you need it."

Was that flirting? Sex might not be part of the plan, but flirting was still on the table?

The power had shifted between them again. He held the money, but she had all the know-how. He did as she said, kicking his feet up onto the footstool and settling back into the chair.

She carefully placed Jane on his chest and again guided his arms around the baby until he was holding Jane tightly. Trish's touch—her fingers moving over his muscles—was warm, strong, *soft*.

He was *not* going to sleep with her. But it would be helpful in accomplishing that noble goal if she didn't touch him. "What if I drop her?" he whispered as Trish's fingers trailed off his forearms, searing him with her warmth.

"You won't." She was close to him then, almost close enough to kiss. But he'd just promised—no funny business. She patted the baby's head. "I'll be back. If she wakes up, just sing to her, okay?"

"Hurry," he told her, trying to sound as if this were all no big deal. "Take a cab. I'll pay for it."

There was a moment when their gazes met—a moment when something shifted between them. She looked down at him with a mixture of confusion and…tenderness?

Then she was gone, walking out the door and hurrying away.

He prayed she'd come back.

He couldn't do this without her.

Three

"What the *hell* am I doing?"

"Sorry?" the cabbie asked in a heavily accented voice.

"Oh—nothing," Trish mumbled, turning her attention back out the window. She had only been in cabs a few times, when going to a symposium with a professor or something. Single travelers probably didn't randomly mutter to themselves.

But, seriously—what the hell was she doing? Moving in with a hot, sweet, *rich* man to take care of his niece? During the last month of her collegiate career? While she was supposed to be organizing the back-to-school drive?

For how much money?

Trish realized she was looking at her fingers, which were slowly counting off the twenty thousand dollars she was going to earn. She ran out of fingers and started over. That was five thousand dollars a week. A week! She didn't earn that much in five months with two jobs.

Twenty grand. That was more than she made in a year, if she didn't count the scholarships—which she tended not to do, since the scholarships didn't buy food or keep the lights on.

And Longmire—Nate—had just thrown that number out.

Along with that *other* number. Two hundred fifty thousand dollars.

Trish stared at her fingers, trying to process the magnitude of that number. Good lord, what her charity could do with that kind of money! New backpacks, shoes and winter coats for every kid on the rez and possibly a few other rezs as well. She could get new sports equipment and fund the afternoon snack in the schools and maybe even get some computers.

It was like a dream come true. Even the part where the hot, rich man was asking her to basically live with him. That was definitely the stuff of dreams. Her dreams, to be specific.

She pinched herself, just to be sure.

The cab pulled up in front of her apartment. "Wait, please," she requested as she got out. The landlady was sitting on her porch, making her disgust for Trish obvious. "Hello, Mrs. Chan," Trish said.

"You leaving?" Mrs. Chan demanded. It was her usual greeting. "You not leaving, you pay more rent. I get $1,900 a month for such nice place, but you only pay me $350."

"Yes, that was the lease we signed," Trish replied. "You get another $450 from the government." Mrs. Chan's "nice place" was a five-hundred-square-foot "garden apartment," which was another way of saying "one step above a root cellar"—only mustier. It'd been furnished, which was helpful when a girl couldn't afford even thrift-store furniture and had no way to get it home, anyway, but it was a combo living-bedroom and bathroom-kitchen. Two rooms in a hole in the ground. Not exactly the lap of luxury and nothing like Nate's elegant Victorian.

But, thanks to the subsidies, it'd been a place Trish could afford and it'd been her own. For the first time in her life, she hadn't had to wait for a bathroom and hadn't had at least two other kids in her bed with her. It hadn't been freezing in the winter and the water always worked. For the past five glorious years, she'd been able to breathe.

"You should pay more," Mrs. Chan sniffed. "My daughter—a *lawyer*—says so." This conversation happened on autopilot.

"Mrs. Chan, you get your wish today."

"What?" The older lady sat up straight and suddenly a bright smile graced her face. "You leaving?"

"I'm leaving. I have a…" She didn't know how to describe the situation. "I have a new place."

"You leave now?"

Trish turned back to where the cab was waiting. It felt too decadent, letting the meter run. "Yup. Right now. I just came back for my things."

"Oh, my." Honest to God, Mrs. Chan batted her eyelashes at Trish. "You such a sweet girl. I always like you."

Trish managed not to roll her eyes, but it took a lot of effort. "Can I get my deposit?"

Some of the sweetness bled out of Mrs. Chan's face. It wasn't like Trish needed the money right now—how weird was it to think *that*?—but she couldn't not get it. It was her $350. Getting the deposit money scraped together had practically taken an act of God—and a favor from her stepfather. She could pay him back now.

"I mail to you," Mrs. Chan finally said.

"Fine. I'll leave my address. I have to go pack."

She unlocked her door as Mrs. Chan rhapsodized about how Trish was "such a sweet girl." This wouldn't take long. She had no furniture to move—even the coffeepot that was possibly as old as she was had come with the apartment.

She started shoving clothes into laundry bags. The books took several trips and then the only thing left was her one true luxury—a laptop. True, it was an old laptop. She didn't particularly like to pull it out when there were people around because the last thing she needed were more funny looks.

But it was a computer and she owned it free and clear and that was what counted.

Forty minutes was all it took to erase the signs of her five years in this dank little apartment. The cabbie helped her load the last bag into his trunk and then they were off, back to the historical Victorian that contained a billionaire and a baby.

There was no going back. Mrs. Chan wouldn't let her come back, not without another grand in rent money every month. Trish was committed now.

The enormity of what she was doing hit her again. Oh, God. She was moving in. With Nate Longmire. Who was out of her league and yet also adorably clueless about small children.

Instead of panicking, she forced herself to make a list. She had so much to do. Explain what had happened to her bosses. Call home and make sure her mom had her new address. Finish her degree.

Live under the same roof as Nate Longmire. He who promised not to sleep with her.

Which was just fine. She did not want to be seduced. Not in the least. Seduction always came with the risk of pregnancy and that was a risk she was not willing to take.

Except…

She had the feeling that if she'd had her wits about her, she could have gotten a million dollars out of him, he was so desperate. But that felt wrong, too.

She'd gone in there for the money, but she didn't want to take advantage of him. Not after watching him struggle to keep his composure as he talked about his family.

Damn her helpful nature. As bad an idea as this was, she couldn't say no and leave him and that poor girl in such obvious distress. Mixing milk in with the formula? Good lord. That baby had probably only been a day or two away from a visit to the emergency room.

Rosita was waiting for the cab. She hurried down the wide stairs and rushed through the gate as Trish unloaded all of her worldly possessions. "Oh, good—you've come back," she said as she handed over a credit card to the cabbie.

"I promised I would."

"They're still sleeping," Rosita went on. "*Ay mia*, this is the most quiet we've had in weeks."

"Will you help me unload? I don't even know where I'm going to be sleeping."

"I made you up a bed. This way, please."

Hefting one of her duffels over her shoulder, Trish followed the maid inside. She paused to peek into the parlor. The man and the baby hadn't moved. Nate still had a firm hold of Jane. The little girl was curled against him, breathing regularly. And Nate?

God, it wasn't fair that he should look so good, so sweet, sleeping like that. It almost made Trish's heart hurt. She'd helped raise nine other babies—and she couldn't remember seeing any father in her house holding his child. She liked to think that, once upon a time, her father had held her before he pulled up stakes and came to San Francisco.

She knew that many men cared for their children. But Jane wasn't even Nate's child—and he was still trying his hardest.

No. She was not going to crush on him. This was not about her attraction to Nate Longmire, no matter how wealthy and good-looking and easy to talk to he was. This was about funding her charity for the foreseeable future and making sure that little girl was well cared for. Trish had too much to do to allow an infatuation to creep into her life and that was final. They'd both agreed to the plan and she would stick by that plan come hell or high water.

She followed Rosita up the stairs. This time, she was able to actually look around. The staircase was a magnificent creation that, at the landing, broke into two sets of stairs, one on each side of the wall. The whole place was so clean it almost glowed in the early evening light. Expensive-looking art—some of it old-looking oil paintings, some of it framed movie posters from schlocky old movies she'd never heard of—decorated the walls in coordinating frames. The walls were a pale green, cool and refreshing, with coordinating chairs in the landing.

Oh, yeah, this was much fancier than anything she'd ever lived in before. This was even fancier than the hotel she'd stayed in for the *Glamour* award in New York. That'd been a very nice hotel—a Marriott—but this? This was officially the lap of luxury. And it was Nate's.

Rosita took the staircase to the right and Trish followed. She wondered if she might go up to the attic—she'd be out of the way there—but Rosita led her down the hall on the second floor.

"That is Señor Nate's room," Rosita said, pointing to the other side of the hallway. "It runs the length of the house. The nursery and the guest room are on this side. Here we are." Rosita opened the first door on her right.

Wait—what? She was going to be right across the hall from him? That felt…close. Too close. He would be too accessible.

But that flash of panic was quickly overridden by the room Rosita led her into. "Oh, my," Trish breathed. A huge, beautiful room awaited her. She'd never had a beautiful room before. The wallpaper was a deep blue-and-cream floral pattern. An actual chandelier hung in the middle. The room had a small bay window that held two sitting chairs and a small table. To one side was a fireplace with deep blue glazed tiles. A flat-screen television hung over the mantel, which was decorated with small vases and figurines. And on the other… "That's an amazing bed."

"Yes. Señor Nate's mother prefers this room when she is able to visit."

The bed was huge. At least a queen-size with four posts that reached up almost to the level of the chandelier, the whole thing was draped with gauzy fabric. The bed was made up with color-coordinating pillows and a down comforter that looked so light and fluffy Trish couldn't wait until she could sleep in it.

Alone. She would be sleeping in that bed *alone*. That was the plan.

Except all the dreams she'd been having for the past two weeks came crashing back down on her head. Nate would be right across the hall, no longer a fantasy, but a flesh-and-blood man who had, in no uncertain terms, said he needed her.

Oh, this was going to be a long, hard month.

"The bathroom, miss," Rosita said. "It connects with the nursery."

"Okay, good." That way, she wouldn't have to walk into the hall in the middle of the night in her T-shirt and boxer shorts and run the risk of stumbling into Nate Longmire. Because that would be terrible. Awful. She was just sure of it.

Her head began to spin. This was too much. Too much money. Not her life. She didn't get paid this kind of cash to watch a billionaire's baby while sleeping in a guest room that was far bigger and cleaner than any other place she'd ever lived.

Her knees wobbled and she sat heavily on the bed. Of course it was soft and comfortable. And it was hers. Hers for the month.

"Tell me about him," she said to Rosita. The maid's eyebrows jumped. "I just agreed to move into his house and I really don't know…anything." She'd done her homework a few weeks ago and yes, he'd shared that little moment down in the parlor. But suddenly that wasn't enough.

Because there'd been huge holes in his biography online. The lawsuits he'd filed—and won. He'd sued a woman named Diana Carter because she'd claimed that half of SnAppShot was hers and had tried to sell it. They'd been old college friends, according to the filings. There were rumors that they'd been more, but that was it—just rumors. And Nate had run her into the ground.

But those were dry legal texts. Anything else that might have provided context about what went on between "old college friends" was simply not there. The information was conspicuous in its absence.

"Señor Nate? He is a good man. Quiet, not messy. Does not make me uncomfortable. Very polite."

"Okay, good." That was mostly how he'd come across during their meeting at the coffee shop. Well, maybe except the messy part.

"He likes to sleep late and he drinks maybe too much coffee," Rosita added in an entirely motherly sounding voice. "But I do not mind. He pays me very well and the work is not too hard. Mostly cooking, cleaning and laundry. It is a very good job."

"Does he...I mean to say, will there be other guests? Who spend the night?" She didn't know why she'd asked that question, but it was out there and there was nothing she could do about it now. She felt her cheeks flush.

It was a matter of self-preservation, that was all. If other people were going to be in and out of this house, that was something she needed to know for Jane's sake. She'd have to lock both her and Jane's doors to make sure no "guests" accidentally wandered into the wrong room. It had nothing to do with not wanting to see Nate going into his bedroom with someone else and closing the door behind them.

"Ay, no! Señor Nate keeps to himself. His helper—

Stanley," she said, drawing the name out in an unflattering way, "he will sleep on the couch sometimes, down in the media room. That is only when they are working on a project. But no. No other guests."

"Stanley—does he have a lot of tattoos, a horrible sense of fashion and big holes in his ears?"

Rosita nodded. "I do not like him. He is loud and messy and rude. But Señor Nate says he is a good man, so I cook for him when he comes over."

Yeah, that pretty much summed up the man Trish had talked to at the office. Loud, messy and rude. "Anything else you think I should know?"

Rosita stepped back and gave Trish the once-over. "No, miss. Just that I'm glad you've taken the position. I…" her voice dropped to a whisper. "I do not care for children. Never had one of my own. They make me nervous," she admitted with an awkward laugh. "That is why this was such a good job. Other people, they want you to look after the children and I…I am no good at it. And it is far too late for me to suddenly become good at it. You understand? It would be hard to find another position as good as this one and I am getting too old to start over."

Trish patted Rosita's arm. Being a woman who currently had no desire to have children, she understood. Some people just didn't like babies. Oftentimes, Trish had to wonder if that included her own mother. Why else would she have left her oldest to care for each new infant?

"No worries. I'm going to unpack a little and then check on them." She looked at the clock beside the bed. Even the clock was fancy—a built-in dock for smartphones and more plugs than she recognized. If only she had a smartphone to dock there. "They've probably got another forty minutes or so before they wake up."

Rosita started to leave but paused at the door. "Miss? I do all the cooking. Anything special you like?"

Trish blinked at her. She was not a gourmet cook. She existed on the cheapest groceries she could afford, and those usually came from corner markets and little shops that carried ethnic foods. Her big splurge was, once a week, buying a nice cup of coffee. If she got really wild, she might eat two whole packets of ramen noodles for dinner. She did not dine at nice restaurants. She didn't even dine at bad ones.

The prospect of this nice woman cooking her food was beyond Trish's comprehension. "I'll eat anything."

Rosita nodded and closed the door behind her.

Trish flopped back onto the bed and stared up at the gauzy canopy. This was, hands down, the craziest thing she'd ever done. Moving in with a billionaire. What the hell?

But already it was hard to think of Nate as just the Boy Billionaire, not when she'd seen him so upset over his family and napping with his niece. She hadn't just moved in with a billionaire. She'd moved in with *Nate*.

She forced herself to stop thinking about the way his very nice arm muscles had tightened under her touch and the way certain parts of her own body had tightened in response. *If* she allowed herself to dwell on those moments—and that was a pretty darned big *if*—well, those thoughts were best kept for after everyone had gone to bed in their separate bedrooms, with all doors safely shut.

Right now, she had things to do. Moving quickly, she unpacked her meager wardrobe. The room had a closet that was almost as big as her kitchen/bathroom in the basement of Mrs. Chan's house, and all the hangers were those fancy padded ones wrapped in satin. Her second-hand clothes looked jarringly out of place on them.

She put her laptop on the table in the window—the little nook would be a wonderful place to do her work—and lined up her books on a built-in bookshelf on the far side of the canopy bed. Finally, she was unpacked.

Time to get down to business. She pulled off her boots and considered her options. Baby duty required wash-and-wear clothes and her professional outfit wasn't it.

As she stripped down to her underwear, she thought about what Rosita had said. Nate was quiet, kept to himself. He didn't bring women home with him. And, aside from Stanley, who slept on the couch, he didn't bring men home with him, either.

Trish threw on the Wonder Woman T-shirt and a pair of jeans, and then removed her earrings and braided her hair back so that it couldn't be yanked by small hands. She was not going to think about Nate and whom he did or did not bring home with him. It was none of her business whom he slept with, as long as he didn't—what had Rosita said? As long as Nate didn't make Trish "uncomfortable."

He'd promised. No sex.

During the month.

Which left what might happen after the month as something of an open question.

Trish shook her head and forced herself to think about the real reason she was here—Jane, the baby. The poor girl.

God, Trish didn't want to be a mother again so soon, not to someone else's child, but…Jane needed her and Nate needed her. And Trish—she needed a well-funded charity that could make a huge difference in her people's lives.

Just a month. She was a temporary nanny. That was the plan.

She opened her door and, barefoot, peeked into the nursery. Rosita had done an admirable job in the hour and a half since Trish had last seen the nursery, but the place was still a mess. Boxes and suitcases were stacked against the walls, baby things spilling out of them. The playpen was almost in the middle of the room and—wait. She stepped around it. A pair of formal sitting chairs—much like the ones in her room, only in a deep rose color—sat in the bay window. That, in itself, wasn't that remarkable.

But one of the chairs had a suitcase that had clearly been used as a footstool. A used coffee cup sat on the little table and a phone—she assumed it was Nate's—was next to it. The whole area looked rumpled, much like Nate had when she'd showed up.

Oh, dear God—no wonder that man was so tired. He'd been sleeping in the chair to be closer to Jane.

She shook her head. He had *no* idea what he was doing, but he was doing his best. She'd work on the nursery tomorrow. There wasn't even a changing table. She'd have to ask if Nate could afford to get a crib, a table and another dresser...

She caught herself. Of course Nate could afford that. Hello, Boy Billionaire who'd just thrown close to three hundred thousand dollars at her. A couple of thousand on some furniture wasn't anything to him.

She left the mess behind and went downstairs to the parlor. She studied the room. For being a tech billionaire, there was very little actual tech in this room. Instead, old toys were artfully arranged on the built-in bookcases around a fireplace with an elegant floral pattern done in bright blue tiles. The mantel that went over it was hand-carved and polished to a high shine. And there, in a place of honor, was Superman #1 in a glass case.

Earlier, when she'd seen the distress Jane was in, Trish had acted without thinking. Her instincts were to get the baby changed and clothed and fed and napping in quick succession.

There was a distinctive possibility that she *might* have been bossing a billionaire around.

But now the situation was not as dire. The baby was resting. Nate was asleep. She didn't know if she could walk in there and pluck Jane off his chest or if that would be crossing a line she shouldn't cross. She really shouldn't touch him. Not like she'd already touched him. No more touching. Touching was not part of the plan.

As she was debating doing that or going back and showing Rosita how to make the formula properly, Nate's eyes fluttered open. He saw her standing there and blinked a few times.

"Hey, Wonder Woman," he mumbled as his long legs stretched out.

"I'm not really a superhero," she felt obligated to remind him.

That got her a sleepy grin. Oh, my. Yes, Nate Longmire could be quite attractive. "You came back."

"I keep my word." She paused. "Listen, about the money…"

His eyes widened. "What about it? Not enough?"

"No—no—it's just—that's an insane amount of money. You don't have to pay me that much. Really. I hadn't even considered the room and board as part of the agreement. And the room—it's really nice. I mean, that alone is worth—"

"Don't worry about it," he sighed as his eyelids drifted shut again. "We agreed. I keep my word, too."

He couldn't be serious. She hadn't been negotiating, not really. She'd just been too stunned to tell him no earlier. "But—"

"The deal is done." His voice was harder now—the same voice he'd used when he had refused to take *no* for an answer. "Not open to renegotiation, Trish."

She tried very hard not to glare at him. "Fine. I have a favor to ask."

One eyelid opened back up. She could almost see him thinking, *another favor?* "Yes?"

"I need to borrow a phone so I can call my family and

tell them where I'm at and I haven't seen a landline in here."

"I don't have a landline," he said as if she'd observed that he didn't have any woolly mammoths in the closets. Both lids swung up in a look of total confusion. "You don't have a phone?"

"Nope." Shame burned her cheeks. She lived in the most technologically advanced city in quite possibly the entire world—and didn't even own a cell phone. "I have a laptop," she said, desperate not to sound pathetic. "I assume you have Wi-Fi or something I can log into, to finish my classwork?"

He regarded her for a minute. She got the feeling he was fully awake now.

"You need a phone."

"I'm fine, it's just that—"

"No, you need a phone," he said with more force. "In case of an emergency. I'll have Stanley get you one. I've cleared most of my schedule, but I have a few events I need to attend and you need to be able to get ahold of me."

"Nate…"

She was going to tell him he absolutely could not buy her a phone. She had existed for twenty-five years without a mobile device just fine. He was already giving her too much.

But when she said his name, something in his eyes changed—deepened. And all those things she was going to tell him floated away like the fog.

"You are too generous," she said, unable to make her voice sound like a normal version of herself. She could never pay him back, not in a million years. "You're giving me too much. I'm not…" *worth it.*

She almost said it out loud but managed not to.

His eyebrows lifted and he opened his mouth and she was suddenly very interested in what he was about to say, but Jane awoke with a start and a cry. Her head lifted up and crashed back into Nate's shoulder. "Ow," he said. "You've got a hard head, Janie girl."

"Here." Trish strode into the room and lifted Jane out of his arms. "I told you that you wouldn't drop her."

"I bow to your superior knowledge," he said working his head from side to side.

She caught a whiff of stale milk. *Old* stale milk. Nate Longmire was on the verge of curdling before her very eyes. "I don't want to tell you what to do..."

He looked up at her, a curious grin on his face. "Don't let that stop you. What?"

"You might consider a shower."

An adorable blush turned his cheeks pink, then red. "That bad?"

She wrinkled her nose at him. "Go. I've got Jane."

He got to his feet and leaned in. For a blistering second, she thought he was going to kiss her. He was going to kiss her and she was going to let him and that was the stupidest thing she'd ever thought because she did not let people kiss her. She just didn't.

He pressed his lips to the top of Jane's head, nestled against Trish's shoulder. Then he straightened up. "Thank you."

This was the closest she'd been to him. Close enough to feel the warmth of his body radiating in the space between them. Close enough to see the deep golden flecks in his brown eyes, no longer hidden behind the hipster glasses. "I haven't done anything yet."

"You're here. Right now, that's everything."

Even though Jane was waking up and starting to fuss at still being swaddled in the blanket, Trish couldn't pull away from the way his eyes held hers.

"You don't have to buy me a phone." It came out as a whisper.

The very corner of his mouth curved up and he suddenly looked very much like a man who would seduce his temporary nanny just because he could. "And yet, I'm going to, anyway."

Trish swallowed down the tingling sensation in the back of her throat. This was Nate after a nap? What would he be like after a solid night's sleep?

And how the hell was she going to resist him?

The baby saved her. Jane made an awful noise and Nate reeled back in horror. "Um...yeah. I'll just go shower now." He stepped around her and all but ran toward the door.

"Coward," she called out after him. "You're going to have to learn sometime!"

"Can't talk, in the shower!" he called back. It sounded like he was laughing.

Trish sighed. "Come on, sweetie," she said to the baby. "It's you and me for the month."

She needed this baby—needed the constant reminder of why she didn't sleep with anyone and especially not with the man who was paying her a salary. She was not going to get caught up in Nate Longmire being an atypical billionaire who looked at her like she was the answer to his prayers, even if she was—in a strictly nanny-based sort of way, of course.

Thank God for dirty diapers.

Four

Nate stood under the waterfall showerhead with his forehead slowly banging against the tiled wall.

When had an easy plan, such as to not sleep with a nanny, suddenly become something that seemed so insurmountably difficult? He didn't seduce people. And when people tried to seduce him—like that woman at the last talk he'd given, the one where he'd met Trish—he managed to sidestep around it.

What was it about Trish Hunter that had him struggling to keep his control in his own home?

It's not like he was a prude. Okay, he sort of was, but it wasn't because he didn't like sex. He did. A lot. But sex was...it was opening yourself up to another person. And that he didn't like. Not anymore.

He didn't pick up women and he didn't get picked up. It was a holdover from a long, painful adolescence, where he'd learned to take care of himself because he sure as hell wasn't going to get much help from anyone else. And yes, it was the fallout from Diana. He wasn't going to put himself in that kind of position again if he could help it. Better to stick it out alone than open himself to that kind of inside attack again.

He turned the cold knob up another three notches.

It didn't help.

He wasn't innocent. College had been good for him on

a couple of different levels. He'd started this company. Started dating. He'd gone to MIT, where no one knew about Brad Longmire or his football championships. Nate had no longer been Brad's little brother. He'd been Nate.

And what was more, he wasn't the biggest geek on campus, not at MIT. He'd blended. For the first time in his life, he'd belonged. He'd filled out, started growing facial hair and gotten lucky a few times. He'd met Diana...

No. He wasn't going to think about that mess. All the paperwork was signed, sealed and approved by the judge. He didn't care if she was trying to get ahold of him again. He was *done* with her.

But Trish...

His hand closed around his dick as Trish's face appeared behind his closed eyes, smiling down at him from where she'd stood in the doorway. She'd looked like an angel as he'd blinked the nap out of his eyes. He'd swear there was a glow around her. And then? She'd tried to give the money back. She could ask him for a million dollars and he'd happily sign the check tomorrow, as long as she stayed and kept Jane happy and healthy.

She hadn't. She'd tried to give some back.

As he stroked himself, he thought of the way she'd been looking at him when he woke up—one arm leaned against the doorjamb, her Wonder Woman–clad breasts no longer hidden behind a respectable jacket. She'd looked soft and happy and glad to see him.

He. Would. Not. Sleep with. Her. He'd given his word. Not for the month, anyway. After that...

After that, he'd ask her out. Ask her to stay—not for the baby, but for him. They'd talk and he'd kiss her and then he'd lead her up to his room and they'd fall into bed together, hands everywhere. Lips everywhere. He wouldn't be able to keep his hands off her.

She'd be on top of him, stripping that superhero shirt off, her thighs gripping him as he thrust up—

Groaning, he reached a shuddering conclusion. *Hell*. It was going to be a long month.

He let the water run on cold for a few more minutes until he was sure he had the situation under control. He'd been in control for years now. He could handle a beautiful young woman living under his roof, no problem.

He was drying off when he heard something—a high, trilling sound that seemed different from all the screaming that Jane had been doing in the past week but was just as loud.

Oh, no. The baby—he shouldn't have taken a shower, not while she was awake. What had he been thinking? Nate wrapped the towel around his waist and shot out of his bathroom, running across the hall toward the sound.

He slipped around the corner to find Trish sitting on the floor with Jane—bouncing the baby on her knee?

"What's wrong?" he demanded.

"What?" Trish looked up and her eyes went wide. "Oh! Um…"

Jane made that noise again and a sick dread filled him. He'd told his mom he couldn't do this. But what choice did he have, really? "What's wrong with her?"

"She's fine," Trish said in a reassuring voice. "We're playing. That's a happy noise." Her gaze cut to his chest— then to the towel—and then back up.

"It…is?" He was wearing a *towel*. And nothing else. He grabbed at it so fast that he almost knocked it loose and suddenly he was very aware that flashing his new nanny probably invalidated any promise, written or spoken, not to have sex with her.

He did the only thing he could do—he stepped to the side, so that his body was on the other side of the doorway.

"It is," Trish replied. "She's had a good nap and a clean

diaper and I bet this is the best she's felt in a little while. Isn't it, sweetie?" she said to the baby. Then she leaned forward and blew a raspberry on Jane's tummy.

The baby squealed in delight and Trish laughed. It was a warm, confident noise.

Then she looked up at him, her full lips still curved up with happiness. "We're fine, if you want to—you know—put on clothes."

"Right, right." Feeling like a first-class idiot, he ran back to his room and threw on some shorts. What the hell was wrong with him? Seriously. That had bordered on totally disastrous—much worse than knocking a coffee into her lap. He absolutely could not afford to do anything to drive her away.

He dug out some clean clothes. In any other situation, he might have called Stanley for advice on what to wear—but what the hell. She'd already seen him at his worst.

Oh, Lord—what had he done? He should have held out. He should have hired a grandmother who was as wide as a bus and had whiskers or something. Not a beautiful young woman who was going to drive him mad with lust. Who was going to challenge him.

He forced himself to run a few lines of code through his mind as he gathered up his very dirty clothes and dumped them in the hamper. The original code to SnAppShot. He knew it by heart. That code was like a security blanket. Whenever he couldn't sleep—which was often—he'd mentally scroll through that code.

Then he got a clean pair of jeans and, after a moment's consideration, his Superman T-shirt. Superman and Wonder Woman, saving the universe one baby at a time. Stanley wouldn't approve, but what the hell.

This time, Nate walked with a purpose back to the nursery. Trish now had the baby on the floor and appeared to be tickling her feet. Whatever she was doing, Jane was kicking and wriggling and making that loud, not-crying noise again.

This was okay, this noise. If Trish said it was okay, it was okay. Loud and unsettling, but okay.

She looked up at him from the floor, where she was lying on her side and had her head propped up on one hand. "You look…good. Nice shirt."

He felt his cheeks get hot. "Couldn't have been much worse, I suppose?"

"It can always be worse," Trish replied. Her eyes darted back down to his chest. Almost unconsciously, he stood up straighter. It'd been one thing for her to stare while he'd been wet and basically naked. But was she checking him out?

She dropped her gaze and he swore the color of her cheeks deepened. "So…"

He leaned forward. "Yes?"

"Jane's going to need a few more things," Trish said in a rush.

"Like what?"

Trish stood and lifted Jane onto her hip with that practiced air. "Everything. This room is a disaster, you know. Were you sleeping in the chair?"

Nate looked over the nursery. The place was still a wreck—and that got his mind firmly back into the here and now and far away from whether or not Trish might have liked what she'd seen a few minutes ago. "Well, yeah. Rosita doesn't live here. She goes home at six most days and comes in at ten because I sleep late. And I was just afraid…"

"That you wouldn't hear her?"

"Or SIDS or something," he agreed. "Elena—Jane's mother—was worried about SIDS, I remember that." God, it was almost too much to bear. He'd liked Elena. She kept Brad grounded and had told Nate to keep the beard because it made him look a little like Ben Affleck and that couldn't be a bad thing, Nate had figured.

But Elena and Brad were gone and Nate was suddenly the guardian of their daughter.

He leaned against the playpen for support.

"You okay?" Trish asked.

"I just...I can't believe they're not coming back, you know? To just have them up and disappear out of my life like *that*?" He snapped his fingers.

"I know." Trish stepped into him and put her free hand on his shoulder. The same fingers that just a few hours ago had skimmed over his skin, making sure he could hold his niece, were now a reassuring hold on him. Without thinking about it, he reached up and covered her hand with his.

"Do you?" He had no business asking—and even less business asking while she was touching him—while he was touching her back. Even if that touch was a reassuring touch, full of comfort and concern and almost no lust at all.

"I do." Then, mercifully, she released her hold on him. She switched Jane to her other hip—the one closer to him—and leaned so the little girl's head was touching him.

Weirdly, that was what he needed. He didn't have his brother or sister-in-law anymore, but he had Jane. And it was his duty to take care of this little girl. He wasn't married and he hadn't foreseen having children anytime soon, but...she was his flesh and blood.

He was a father now. He had to stand tall for her. For them both.

He tilted his head to the side and looked at Trish out of the corner of his eye. She was watching him with concern. Jane made a squealing noise and Nate jumped. "Yeah, that's why I was sleeping in here," he said, getting himself back together. "She makes all these weird noises that don't seem normal..."

"They are," Trish said calmly. "How old is she?"

"Almost six months."

Trish stepped back from him and twirled around. Her mouth open wide, Jane let out a squeal of delight. Trish stopped spinning and looked in her mouth. "Hmm. No teeth yet. But if she's having trouble sleeping, that might be part of it."

"Oh. Okay." Teething. Yet another thing he didn't have a clue about. "That's normal, right?"

Trish grinned at him, then unexpectedly spun again, making Jane giggle. Yes—definitely a giggle. "Right. We've got to get this room whipped into shape."

"One moment." He pulled out his phone and video-messaged Stanley.

Stanley's face appeared. "What? It's after seven."

"And hello to you, too. I need you to go shopping. Start a list," Nate said. "Company phone for Ms. Trish Hunter."

Off to his side, Trish sighed heavily, but she didn't protest.

"And?" Stanley said.

Nate looked at Trish. "And?"

"A crib, changing table, dresser drawers, a rocker-glider chair, stroller, car seat, high chair, size two diapers, more formula."

"Did you get all that?" Nate asked.

"Is that the girl? She came here first. I had to send her your way," Stanley said in that absent-minded way of his that meant he was taking notes.

"Yes," Nate said. "She took the position. Also, I need you to do the due diligence on One Child, One..." he could not remember the last part of her charity's name. It just wasn't there.

"World. One Child, One World," Trish helpfully supplied. Her eyes had gotten big and round again.

"One Child, One World," Nate told Stanley. "I'm going

to be making a donation for two hundred fifty thousand dollars. Also, please put Ms. Hunter on the payroll."

"Salary?" Stanley said.

"Twenty thousand for one month."

There was a moment's pause in which Stanley's eyebrows jumped up. "Can I have a raise?"

This time, Nate did snort. For as much as he paid Stanley, the man was constantly haranguing him for more. "No."

"She must be *highly* qualified," he said in that distracted way again. "Good body, too."

Nate cringed. "She's also listening."

After a frozen pause—his eyes wide in horror—Stanley cleared his throat. When he spoke again, he did so in his most professional voice. "When do you need this by?"

Nate looked at Trish and was surprised to see that she was trying not to laugh. "As soon as possible," she managed to get out.

"Right. Got it." Stanley ended the call.

Nate stood there, staring down at his screen. He really didn't know what to do next. Trish did have a good body. And an excellent sense of humor about it, too.

"Well. That wasn't awkward at all."

He grinned. "The least awkward conversation ever, possibly."

They stood there. There was tension in the room, but it wasn't the kind that normally had him tripping over his words or his feet. He was comfortable with her. And, despite all the not-awkwardness, she seemed pretty okay with him. Enough to send him to the shower because he reeked.

"Señor Nate?" Rosita called up from downstairs. "Dinner is on the table. Do you need me for anything else? It is after seven o'clock..."

Nate glanced at Trish, who shook her head. The past few nights, when Rosita had fled from the house at exactly six—leaving Nate all alone with Jane—he'd been filled with a sense of dread that was far heavier than anything else he'd ever had to overcome.

But not tonight. A sense of calm brushed away the nagging conviction that he couldn't do this. And that calm was named Trish.

"I think we're going to make it," he called back. "See you on Monday?"

"Yes," Rosita called back, sounding relieved.

The sound of the front door shutting echoed through the house. "She's a very good cook," he felt like he had to explain, "but she doesn't really like kids."

"So she said. And Stanley?"

"Don't feel too sorry for him. He gets fifty bucks an hour." Her face paled a bit—no doubt, she was thinking about the twelve fifty an hour she'd earned as of this morning. "I know he's a little rough around the edges, but he's the height of discretion. They both are."

"You value your privacy."

"Doesn't everyone?" Which was a true enough statement, but he knew that wasn't what she was asking.

She'd as much as admitted that she'd dug into his history. But he didn't want to go down that path right now. Just because she was someone he'd like to get to know better and who was technically living under his roof at this very moment didn't mean he had to just open up and share his deepest secrets with her.

So he did the only thing he could do. He changed the subject. "Shall we have dinner? Then I can show you the rest of the house and you can teach me how to make the formula." Because he was going to have to learn it sometime and that was a concrete task that probably wouldn't involve lingering touches or long looks. Hopefully.

Like the long look she gave him right then, punctuated only when she shifted Jane to her other hip. There was something in her eyes, as if she didn't believe what he'd just suggested. "Yes," she said after that measured gaze, "We shall."

Five

Trish lay in bed, not sleeping. This house sounded different. She was used to the shuffling of Mrs. Chan over her head and the blaring of the evening news. But Nate's house?

This place was quiet. Nearly silent. In the distance, a foghorn sounded.

She'd never had so much quiet. Funny how it felt loud. Was this why Nate lived here—he could hear himself think?

They'd gone up to the dining room, where the best danged chicken enchilada dinner she'd ever eaten had been waiting for them in a dining room that was not rated for kids. The table had ten chairs and was set upon a thick white shag rug. Trish had suggested that Nate remove the carpeting before Jane started eating solid foods.

And then there'd been the view. Not that she'd been able to see much in the fog, but Nate had said that the floor-to-ceiling glass windows that separated the dining room from the patio had an excellent view of the Golden Gate Bridge. Trish hadn't had a view of anything but the sidewalk in five years. There was even a fenced-in yard with trees and grass. Nate had asked her if he should get a swing set or something for Jane. After that, Nate had showed her the media room and the home gym in the basement.

Trish didn't belong here. This house, the food, everything about Nate was out of her league. Had she really felt like an interloper at San Francisco State University? Good lord. That was nothing compared to finding herself suddenly living in the absolute lap of luxury with a man who took such a vital interest in his niece's welfare.

Trish's current stepfather was a pretty good guy. He supported Pat and the kids still living at home and that counted for a hell of a lot. He'd even loaned Trish the $350 for her security deposit five years ago—and that had only been two years after he'd hooked up with Pat.

But there'd been so many men who'd passed through Pat's and Trish's lives and not one of them had ever taken an interest in the kids. Not someone else's kids, not their own kids. Trish's own father had abandoned them, for crying out loud.

To watch Nate try so hard—care so much—well, it spun her head around. One of the reasons she'd gone out of her way to avoid a relationship, and men in general, was because she didn't want to be saddled raising a child on her own. She knew exactly what kind of sacrifices a baby would require and she was done making them for other people.

But Nate… He'd stood shoulder-to-shoulder with her in the kitchen and made up three bottles of formula until he'd gotten it right and he hadn't complained at all. In fact, they'd wound up laughing together after his first attempt had resulted in something closer to a pancake batter than formula. He'd taken another crack at changing a diaper, too. Willingly.

Not like the man who'd come into her life when Trish had been nine. That year had made her tougher than she knew she could be. She'd decided then that she would protect her little brothers and sisters. She would get her education even if it took her two years longer to graduate and then she would get the hell off that rez. And when she'd made it, she'd do everything she could to make sure that no other kid went hungry.

She would never again be at the mercy of a man.

Which did not explain why she was living in Nate Longmire's home, caring for his niece, completely dependent on him for her meals and money. Taking this position was something so impulsive, so not thought-out, that even her mother, Pat, would be surprised.

She was completely at Nate's mercy right now and all she had to go on was that his maid said he was a good man and he'd promised sex wasn't part of the plan. That was it. She tried to reason that at least Nate had a reference—her mother had hooked up on far less—but it didn't change the fact that, for the first time in her life, Trish had followed in her mother's footsteps. When a good-looking man had said jump, she'd asked how high and tossed everything to the side to take care of another baby.

Trish didn't know what to think anymore. The certainty with which she'd lived her life for the past ten, fifteen years—suddenly, she wasn't so certain that she was absolutely doing the right thing.

Trish went around and around with herself. Then she heard a soft *whump* and she sat up, her ears straining. The clock said one-thirty. She must have drifted off at some point.

Then she heard it, the building whine of a baby who was not quite awake yet. She threw off her covers and hurried through the adjoining bathroom door. She turned on the bathroom light and let the door open enough that she could see her way to the playpen.

Jane had gotten herself loose from her swaddling and was flailing about. "Shh, shh, it's okay, sweetie," Trish said as she picked up the baby. "I'm here. Let's go get a bottle, okay? Let's let Nate sleep."

The moment the words left her mouth, the overhead lights flipped on. Jane flinched and began to cry in earnest.

Blinking hard, Trish spun to see Nate standing in the doorway in a T-shirt and a pair of boxers—not all that different from what she was wearing.

"Everything okay?" he asked in a bleary voice.

"The light—turn it off."

"What?"

"Nate," she hissed in a whisper. "Turn the light off. Please. You're upsetting Jane."

"Oh." He flipped the light off and Jane quieted back down to a pleading whimper. "Was that bad?"

"We should keep it as quiet and as dark as possible during the night." She could see what had happened now. Every time the baby had made a noise, Nate had hopped up and turned on the overhead lights, which had woken Jane up even more. No wonder he hadn't slept.

She realized she was aware of Nate standing there in his boxers—and she didn't like being that aware of him, all sleepy and rumpled and still very attractive. Like a man who'd feel just right curled up against her in bed. Her nipples tightened under her tank top.

No, no—bad. Bad thoughts. She could only hope that, in the dim light, he hadn't noticed. She shifted Jane so the baby covered her breasts and headed toward the door. She kept her voice low. "I've got this. You go back to bed."

He yawned. "Anything I can do to help?"

"Nope. Just going to get her a bottle, get her changed and lay her back down."

Nate scratched the back of his head. "You want me to get the bottle for you?"

She stopped then, not three feet from him. "You're paying me to do night duty, you know." Besides, the odds of him doing something not conducive to getting a baby back to sleep were pretty high.

He looked as if he was going to argue with her, but then he yawned again. "Okay. But you'll let me know if you need me, right?"

"Right." She started walking again, but Nate didn't get out of her way. She was forced to squeeze her body past his in the door frame.

Unexpectedly, he leaned forward and kissed the top of Jane's head. "Be a good girl," he murmured. Then he looked up. He was close enough to touch, except for the infant between them. "You're sure you don't need me?"

An unfamiliar sensation fluttered across Trish's lower back, like static electricity right at the base of her spine. It tightened muscles in unfamiliar areas, sending a dull ache through her body.

"No," she whispered so softly that he was forced to lean forward a bit just to hear her. For some insane reason, she wanted to run her fingers over his beard. She clutched the baby tighter. "I'm…I'm fine. We're fine."

"Good night, Trish." He pushed off and walked back to his room.

It was only when his door was safely shut that Trish sagged against the door frame. "Good night, Nate."

Oh, heavens. One night down.

Twenty-nine nights to go.

Through the fog of the first decent night's sleep in two weeks, Nate heard Jane fuss twice more during the night. Both times, he woke up with a start, his heart pounding in terror. The baby—

But then, both times, he heard the soft footsteps moving around his house and he remembered—Trish. The woman who was taking care of Jane. The beautiful woman who made him think about things he had long ago learned not to think about. Like sex.

And he lay there both times, fighting the urge to get up

and check on Jane—and Trish—because, after all, he *was* paying her to get up in the middle of the night.

He shouldn't have gotten up the first time, but he was still a tad jumpy about the whole situation. And then Trish had been there, her body silhouetted against the dim light from the bathroom like an angel of mercy, come to save him from himself. Her bare shoulders had been haloed with the light and her curves—

He'd almost kissed her. He'd promised he wouldn't and he almost had, anyway. It'd been the sleep deprivation, that was all. He must be too tired to think straight because he knew he could control himself better than that.

So, in a monumental effort of self-control, he stayed in bed, drifting between true sleep and awareness. The first time, the house eventually became quiet again and he slept. But the second time—even though Trish was not being loud—he still heard her moving around downstairs.

He rolled over and looked at the clock. Six-fifty in the morning. Ugh. He normally slept much later than this, until nine or ten. He tried to bury his head in a pillow, but it didn't work.

He pictured Trish moving through his house, Jane on her hip, looking like she belonged here. He remembered the way she'd looked at him when he'd tried to make the bottle of formula—a smile she was trying to hide and a warmth in her eyes that couldn't be hidden.

That warmth—that had to be why he'd not-so-subtly hit on her last night. He was out of practice. He wanted to think that she looked at him like that because there was some interest on her end—the same interest he thought he'd seen in the coffee shop.

Of course, if she knew about what had happened with Diana…maybe she wouldn't look at him like that anymore. It's not like he had to worry about Brad swooping in and charming the pants off Trish, though.

The moment he had that thought, enormous guilt swamped him.

God, he was a mess and because he was such a mess, he'd almost broken his promise to Trish. That wasn't like him.

What if, after last night, she'd changed her mind about staying? What if he'd crossed a line he couldn't uncross? Then he'd be little better than Brad had been, unable to keep it zipped around a woman who should be hands-off. And he'd be on his own with a baby again, trying not to screw things up and probably screwing up, anyway.

Panicked, he dragged his tired butt out of bed and threw on a clean pair of jeans. He'd apologize, that was all. He'd do a much better job of keeping a mental wall between Trish Hunter, his nanny, and Trish Hunter, woman of his fantasies. He was not ruled by his baser urges. He was better than that. He was better than Brad, God rest his soul.

Nate hurried downstairs, trying to come up with a mature, responsible way to apologize for his behavior and failing pretty badly.

He looked in the parlor, but they weren't there. The kitchen was also empty, but there were more used bottles in the sink. It wasn't until he got to the dining room and saw the open doors that he found them.

The fog from the night before had mostly burned off, leaving the world with a hazy glow similar to the most-used filter on SnAppShot. And in the middle of the patio sat Trish. Her hair was long and loose, spilling down over the back of the padded patio chair she occupied. Her feet were bare and kicked up against the railing. She had on a long-sleeved flannel top to ward off the morning chill, so her shoulders were covered, thank God. She'd also added a pair of jeans. Jane was on her lap, a small blanket tucked around her and both were facing out to bay, where the outline of the Golden Gate Bridge was just emerging from the mist. The scene was one of complete and total peace. Trish was rubbing Jane's little tummy and humming again—a tune Nate didn't recognize.

He hesitated. The scene was almost too perfect—there was no way he wanted to kill the moment by stumbling out and opening his mouth. He just wanted to feel the serenity in this moment a little longer. All his anxiety seemed to ease.

"Good morning," she said in that sweet voice of hers.

Nate stepped out onto the patio. Jane rolled in Trish's arm and, grinning a particularly drooly grin, stretched out a hand for him.

This was something new. The baby was actually glad to see him. "Good morning. Long night?"

Trish twisted to look at him over her shoulder, her long hair rippling like silk in water. Her face lit up as she looked at him, as if not only was she not going to hold his midnight madness against him, but she might just welcome a little bit more madness. "I've had longer. God, this is an amazing view."

No more madness. That was the deal. Nate offered his finger to Jane, whose smile got even wider. "She's happy," he said. "I mean—well, you know what I mean. I hadn't seen her happy until you came."

Trish dropped her gaze to the baby's head and smoothed the fine hairs. "A decent night's sleep and a full tummy will do that."

He *had* to make sure Trish stayed. He needed her in a very concrete way that had nothing to do with his attraction to her. "Look, about last night…"

"There's coffee, if you want some. It's not good coffee," she interrupted, turning her gaze back to the bay. "But it *is* coffee. You'll have to show me how to use that machine."

Jane made a cooing noise and turned back to the view, too. But she didn't let go of Nate's finger.

Well. This was awkward. He decided the manly thing to do was to set the record straight. Time to suck up his pride. "I'm sorry that I crossed a line last night. I wasn't all the way awake and—"

She looked up at him again and this time, there was confusion in her eyes. "What line did you cross?"

"I..." he swallowed and dropped his gaze. "I..."

"You wanted to kiss me?"

So. After all these years of being a geek and a klutz and failing at a majority of social interactions involving the opposite sex, he was *finally* going to die of embarrassment. Fitting. "Well, yeah."

She tilted her head, as if she were pondering this admission. "But you didn't."

"Because that was the plan. I don't want to break our deal. You're making Jane happy. I want you to stay the whole month." The words fell out of his mouth in a rush.

"You didn't kiss me. You didn't come into my room in the middle of the night. You aren't trying to force me to do anything I don't choose to do of my own free will."

The way she said it hit him like a slow-swung sledgehammer because no matter how clueless he could sometimes be, even he heard the truth behind those words.

He hadn't done any of those things.

But someone else had.

"I would *never*," he got out, his voice shaking. White hot fury poured through his body at the thought of someone doing any of that to her.

She nodded. "Then I'll stay. A deal's a deal. There's nothing wrong with attraction if we don't act on it."

"Okay. Good." Then what she'd said sunk in. Did she mean his attraction? Or did she mean she was attracted to him, too?

It didn't matter. Because even if she was attracted, she

wasn't going to act on it. Because that was the deal. For the month.

After the month was up...

He looked down and saw a mostly empty coffee cup on the patio table. "I'll get you some more coffee."

"Thanks."

Nate was gone so long that Trish was on the verge of going to look for him. But the early-morning sun had burned off the rest of the fog and the view was simply amazing and this chair was very comfortable and...

And he'd wanted to kiss her. But hadn't.

So she stayed in her chair and played with Jane. The little girl's personality had done a complete 180 in twenty-four hours. Jane was a happy, smiley baby who was definitely teething. "You're a sweetheart, you know that?" Trish cooed to her as the baby bit down on one of her fingers. "I bet you were the apple of your mommy's eye."

A pang of sadness hit her. Jane would never know her mother—and would never remember Trish, either. Trish would be long gone before that could happen. All she could do was make sure that Nate was set up to care for the girl.

And then...

No. She wasn't going to get ahead of herself. Just because Nate was attracted to her didn't mean a damn thing in the long term. The short term was why she was here. She needed to start Jane on solid foods and get some teething rings. But first, Trish was going to make sure the baby stayed up until after the lunch feeding. What this girl needed was a regular sleep schedule, the faster the better.

Finally, Nate re-emerged, a tray in his hands. "Breakfast?" he said, setting the tray down on the small table.

Trish leaned over and saw that he'd assembled bacon, scrambled eggs and toast, in addition to a carafe of coffee—and a fresh bottle of formula. "Oh," she breathed at the sight of all that glorious food. "I wondered what was taking so long."

"It turns out that you make really bad coffee," he said, settling into the other chair. "So while it was brewing, I decided to make breakfast. And I didn't know if Janie needed another bottle or not, so I brought one just the same."

"You cook? I thought that was why you had Rosita." She selected a piece of toast and took a bite. He'd buttered it and everything.

"She's only been with me since I bought the house. Before I sold the company, I couldn't bring myself to spend the money on a cook. It's that frugal Midwestern upbringing. And a man's got to eat. Her cooking is better, but I can get by." He speared a couple of pieces of bacon and said, "Eggs?"

"Yes, please." Trish had another moment of the surreal. Was one of the most eligible bachelors in all of Silicon Valley really making her *breakfast*? How was she supposed to stand strong against this? "This is really good. Thank you."

He nodded in acknowldgment, because his mouth was full of food. They ate in comfortable silence as sunlight bathed the Golden Gate. The neighborhood was waking up. Trish could hear more traffic on the street, and the muffled sounds of voices from the surrounding houses. But the noise still felt distant. "It's so quiet here."

"I worked with a landscape architect to dampen outside noise." He pointed to the trees and shrubs and then at the trailing vines that surrounded the patio. "There are fences on the other side that you can't see—that keep prying eyes out, too. You can't be too careful. You never know what people will try to turn up."

There it was again—another allusion to something that he wanted to keep buried. "Where did you live before you moved here?"

"I had an apartment in the Mission District," he admitted. "Predictable, huh?"

"Very," she agreed. Even the eggs were good. Jane tried to grab a piece of toast, but Trish handed her the bottle instead. She wanted to have a better understanding of the girl before she started feeding Jane things like bread.

"What about you?"

"A 'garden' apartment in Ingleside. I lived there for almost five years—the whole time I've been in the city."

He chewed that over. "So you came here from where, again?"

"Standing Rock reservation. It straddles the line between North and South Dakota. We lived on the South Dakota side." She tried to call up the mental picture of the never-ending grass, but it didn't mesh with the view of the San Francisco Bay she was looking at. "It's a whole bunch of nothing and a few Indians. Our school was one of those portable trailers that someone parked there about twenty years ago." She sighed.

"Wait. You said you were twenty-five."

"I am."

"You didn't go to college until you were twenty?" She must have given him a sharp look because he added, "I mean, I'm just surprised. You're obviously intelligent. I would be less surprised if you'd graduated a year early or something."

She set her plate aside. Her appetite was gone and Jane was getting squirmy. She pulled the baby back into her arms and held the bottle for her. "I suppose if I'd gone to a normal school or had a normal family, I might have. But I didn't."

"No?"

She debated telling him about this part of her life. He was going to be funding her charity for the foreseeable future, after all. Maybe if she could make him understand how bad it really was, he'd be interested in more than just cutting her a check. He might take an active advisory role in One Child, One World. It could be a smart strategic move.

Except...except then he'd know. He'd know everything and when people knew everything, they had a hard time looking at her as Trish Hunter, regular woman. Instead, they looked at her with pity in their eyes or worse—horror. She didn't want his pity. She didn't want anyone's pity. She wanted respect and nothing less.

She considered lying. She could tell him that she'd gotten two years into a mathematics program and decided she just didn't like sines and cosines that much.

But she didn't want to lie to him. He'd been nothing but honest and upfront with his situation. So she decided to gloss over the harsh realities of her life, just a little. Not a lie, but not the painful truth.

"Life's not always fair. For various reasons, I had to miss a couple of years to help out at home." That was the understatement of the century, she thought with a mental snort. Raising her siblings—and burying one—wasn't "helping." It was taking care of *everything*.

He appeared to weigh that statement. "No, life's not always fair. If it were...we wouldn't be here."

"Exactly." She'd still be back in her underground cavern of an apartment, listening to Mrs. Chan berate her for paying such a low rent and counting down the days until she got her master's degree. "Although having a billionaire serve me breakfast on his private patio isn't really all that bad, is it?" She managed a grin. At least her mouth had managed not to add "hot" to "billionaire." Score one for really bad coffee.

"Just making the best of a lousy situation," he agreed. "Better than it was yesterday, I'll say that much."

"Agreed." Yesterday, she'd eaten dry cereal out of the

box—but not too much, because that box had to last her another week.

"What about tomorrow?"

"It's Sunday?"

"Okay," he said, rolling his eyes in a very dramatic way. "Next week, then. We should probably get a schedule set out. You need to finish your degree and I can probably handle Janie on my own for a while…right?"

"You will be fine. You're a quick study."

She swore he blushed at the compliment and danged if it didn't make him look even better. "If you say so. When do you have classes?"

"I managed to get them all on Tuesdays and Thursdays. I worked the other three days, but I guess I'm not doing that anymore right now?"

He shot her a look that could only be described as commandeering and she remembered that, even if he had made her breakfast, he was still a billionaire who had a reputation as being ruthless in business—and that he basically controlled her time. "Right."

"Well, SFSU isn't exactly within walking distance. It'll take me an hour or so to get there by bus, but if I follow the schedule right, I won't—"

"You're not taking the bus," he informed her.

She physically flinched at his harsh tone. "Excuse me?"

"I mean," he said, "it's not a good use of your time to take the bus. Losing you for a couple of extra hours each day just so you can take the bus is unacceptable. I do own a car. You're free to use it."

A car she could use. There was only one problem. "I couldn't do that."

He waved her hands. "You are, at this exact moment, working for me. Your time is valuable to me. I'm not going to let you waste that time because you don't want to borrow my car."

She glared at him. She couldn't help it. "I don't have a license." His eyebrows jumped up, as if that was the last thing he'd expected her to say. "I mean. I've driven, of course. But I…"

He leaned forward, all of his attention focused on her. "Yes?"

"I couldn't afford to take the driving test and there was no hope of being able to afford a car, so what was the point?"

"Then we'll call for a car," he decided. "That's how I travel a lot, anyway."

"No."

"Because it's too expensive?"

"Well, yes," she said her cheeks shooting red. "I can afford the bus." Even with the overwhelmingly generous salary he was paying her, she couldn't start spending money like she had it. She had to make that twenty grand last for as long as possible.

"And I can afford a car service."

She glared at him openly then. "You're not going to make this easy, are you?"

"Are you kidding? This *is* the easy part. I'm paying the tab. I'm the boss. You'll take a car. I'll drive you myself if I have to." She raised an eyebrow. "Once you install the car seat, that is."

"This is ridiculous," she muttered, turning her attention to the meal.

"No, ridiculous is a five million–dollar comic book. This is a wise use of your time."

"You're already paying me too much—housing me, feeding me," she said quietly. "And the phone." She was going deeper into his debt and that feeling left her… unsettled.

He scoffed. "It's not like I'm going to have my private jet fly you the five miles." Then he turned on the most stunning smile she'd ever seen. "The jet is only for trips over ten miles."

She laughed at him, but that smile did some mighty funny things to her—things that spread a warmth through her body that warded off the last of the early-morning chill.

He'd almost kissed her. And she'd almost let him.

"What about you? What's your schedule?"

"I can be home this week, but I have a gala charity function I really should attend next Saturday night. I think the next two Saturdays are also booked. If that works with your schedule."

"That's fine." That'd be three less nights that she had to be around him, because it was becoming very clear that being around Nate Longmire was a dangerous place for her to be.

Because, after less than twenty-four hours, she was already becoming too attached. She'd lived in that hole in the ground for five years and had walked away without a second thought because it was nothing more than a hell-hole with a bed in it. But this place? With the feather beds and beautiful decorating and amazing views and every comfort she'd ever dreamed of growing up?

This place where Nate lived, where Nate slept with a baby on his chest, where Nate made her breakfast and insisted on taking care of her?

It'd be hard to walk away from this, to go back to living in cheap and crappy apartments. To being alone all the time.

To having no one care if she was an hour later on the bus or not.

Trish was in *so* much trouble.

Six

Nate found himself on the phone with the Chair of the School of Social Work at San Francisco State University first thing Monday morning, explaining how he'd poached the chairwoman's best student worker for a nanny position. And then pledging some money to the Social Work program to ease the strain he'd put on the chairwoman's department.

A complete baby's room showed up Monday morning, along with Trish's phone and a passable legal contract codifying their agreement. They both signed with Stanley serving as witness.

Then Nate and Stanley put the furniture together under Trish's increasingly amused direction. Nate let her arrange the room as she saw fit and Stanley followed his lead.

It was only when Trish took Jane downstairs to get her a bottle and try to nap in the quiet of the parlor that Stanley dared open his big mouth. "Dude, she is *hot*."

"It's not like that."

Stanley snorted. "It never is with you. Man, when was the last time you got laid?"

Against his will, Nate felt himself blush. "That's not relevant to the discussion."

"Like hell it's not. And don't try to tell me it's not because you're not into her." Stanley punched him in the arm, which made Nate almost drop the side of the crib he was holding. "I've seen you stick your foot into your mouth around every species of female known to mankind and I've yet to see you actually talk to a woman like you talk to *her*. It's almost like aliens have taken over your body and made you *not* lame or something. And what's even more unbelievable is that she totally seems to be digging you." Stanley shook his head in true shock.

Nate glared at him. He didn't want to particularly own up to the conversation he'd had with Trish at breakfast the other morning, where she'd easily identified how interested he was and conveniently sidestepped whether or not she felt anywhere near the same. "I've stuck my foot in my mouth enough already."

"Yeah?" Stanley looked impressed as they tried to get the crib to lock together like it did in the instructions. "What went wrong? Tell me you didn't stick your tongue down her throat on the first kiss."

"I didn't kiss her," Nate got out. His brain oh-so-helpfully added, *yet.* Yeah, right. "She made her position very clear. No sex."

Stanley whistled. *"Dude."*

"And may I just take this moment to remind you—again—that if I ever hear a word of this conversation even whispered by the press that I'll—"

"Personally turn my ass into grass, yeah, yeah, I got it. You know I can keep my mouth shut." But he looked at Nate expectantly.

If it were anyone other than Stanley...but the man was the closest thing to a confidant that Nate had. "Look, she's an amazing woman. You have no idea."

Stanley chuckled. "No, but I'm getting one."

"But," Nate went on, "we had a deal and you know I won't break a deal."

"Yeah," Stanley said in a pitiable voice, as if this was

the saddest thing he'd ever heard, "I know. You're very reliable like that."

"What about her charity? Did you finish the due diligence?"

"Gosh, gee, I was a little busy freaking out the workers at Babies 'R' Us," he said in an innocent voice. "Apparently, single men who look like I do rarely go shopping for baby things by themselves. So no, not yet. I'll get started after we get this damn crib together. You still going to the event on Saturday?"

"Yeah."

"Remember, I have a family thing. If I set your tux out now, can you get your tie on by yourself?"

Nate debated the odds of that. He didn't think so, but Stanley rarely asked for time off. "Probably."

Stanley nodded, but Nate didn't miss the look of doubt. "You going to take *her*? You know that Finklestein's going to try and set you up with his granddaughter again."

"Oh, God," Nate moaned. He'd forgotten about Martin Finklestein, a pillar of San Francisco's high society who'd become convinced, upon Nate's entry into the billionaires' club, that he and Lola Finklestein were perfect for each other. "I had forgotten. Is it too late to cancel?" He debated telling Stanley about the most recent message he'd gotten from Diana, but decided against it. He was just ignoring her at this point. He didn't need help to pull that off.

Stanley snorted. "Just take Trish."

"And do *what* with the baby? We haven't even gotten to the point where I'm ready to start interviewing other nannies yet and there's no way in *hell* we're going to use that service again."

"Mental note made," Stanley said. "There!" He slid the panel in and the crib stood on its own. "Man, babies are a hassle."

That made Nate laugh. "Dude, you have no idea."

* * *

Trish was trying to get Jane on a sleep schedule, which meant that the baby was supposed to stay awake from whenever she got up until at least one, so, for a couple of hours around lunchtime, Jane was a tad fussy.

And by "a tad fussy," Nate really meant that Jane reverted back to her pre-Trish state of near-constant screaming. He found the noise to be almost unbearable, but Trish would just smile and power through as if baby wailing was music to her ears.

Nate was forced to admit that the payoff was pretty nice. Jane started sleeping from one to three in the afternoon within a matter of days and went from getting Trish up three times a night to two, which meant that everyone—even Nate—was sleeping better.

He even did okay when Trish went to school on Tuesday and Thursday—in a hired car. She only left after she was confident that both Nate and Rosita could fix the formula and Nate could change the diapers. "Call me if you have a problem," she said. "But you can do this."

That she'd said it when Nate was so clearly about to panic was nice enough. But what was even nicer was the way she'd laid her hand on his biceps and given his arm a light squeeze. Then, after kissing Jane's little head, she'd gathered up her bag and headed out to the hired car.

"What do you think?" Nate had asked the little girl.

Jane made a gurgling noise.

"Yeah," Nate had agreed. "I feel the same way."

The day was long. The screaming wasn't too bad and he'd gotten Jane to go down for her nap. That was something he hadn't even gotten close to in the week before Trish showed up.

Still, Nate was waiting for her when the hired car pulled up in front of the house at five-fifteen and Trish got out.

Jane had woken up at two-fifteen and had not been exactly a happy camper without Trish.

"I'm so glad you're back," he said when she walked into the house.

"Rough day? Come here, sweetie." She took Jane from him. "It looks like you're doing okay. She's dressed and everything this time."

Nate blushed. "She's just fussy. I don't know if she's teething or if she just wanted you?"

"Oh, sweetie," Trish said in that soothing voice as she rubbed Jane's back.

Jane buried her tear-streaked face into Trish's neck. Nate was once again struck by the feeling of how *right* the two of them looked together. Trish would never be Elena and God knew that Nate would never be Brad, but life wasn't fair and they were doing the best they could.

Suddenly, he wanted to ask her to go to the gala with him. She'd look amazing in a gown, her arm linked through his as they strode up the steps of the Opera House. That would get Finklestein to back off about Nate settling down with his granddaughter.

Except…Nate was reasonably confident that Trish didn't own a ball gown and that she wouldn't let him buy her one without one hell of a fight.

And there was the problem of Jane. Rosita was back to her happy self now that she was not responsible for Jane's well-being. There was no way Nate could ask his maid to babysit and who else did he trust? Stanley? That wasn't going to happen, either.

So he resigned himself to fending off Finklestein's advances—again.

Once Trish had Jane, Nate called his parents. He knew Joe would be down for a nap, thanks to the meds he was on. Nate resisted the urge to put them on video chat—some things were just beyond his parents. His mom answered.

"Hey, Mom. How are you?"

His mother sniffed. "We're getting by. How are you? How is Jane?"

"Good. Really good. She's teething, but I think she's doing as well as could be expected. I hired the perfect nanny and she's just done wonderfully with Jane. She got the nursery all set up and Jane's even started sleeping better."

"Oh, thank God," Mom said, the relief obvious in her voice. "We've been just worried sick about you two together. Honey, we're so sorry we had to ask you to take Jane, but you know Joe hasn't been dealing with any of this very well and—"

"I know, Mom. But it's going to be okay. Trish is here—that's the nanny. Trish Hunter. She knows what she's doing. I'll send you a couple of pictures later, okay?"

"That would be wonderful, dear."

They talked a bit more about how Joe was doing and how the town was reacting to the loss of one of its golden boys. Then Mom said, "Oh, Joe's up. Honey, we'll talk later and maybe after things calm down here a bit, I'll see about coming out, okay?"

"That'd be good, Mom. I know Jane will be happy to see you again."

"We're so proud of you, Nate," Mom said. It was her usual closing statement, but it hit Nate differently this time.

"I love you, too. Tell Joe I said howdy." He ended the call.

If only he knew what was going to happen next. Obviously, he was going to be a father. But was he going to find love and get married? Would he settle down with Lola Finklestein? Okay, he knew the answer to that one—no.

But...Stanley had been right. Nate didn't talk to a lot of women. Would he just have nannies who helped raise

Jane until she was old enough that he could handle her by himself?

The thought of Lola and other nannies bothered him. Then he thought of how Trish looked in the morning, watching the sunrise with Jane tucked on her lap.

She was only here for a month—less than a month, now. That was the plan.

But after the month was up?

He didn't know.

It wasn't until Thursday afternoon, from the cushy backseat of a hired car on her way back to Nate's house after her classes that Trish used her brand new smartphone to call home. Even with the hired car, it was going to take about forty minutes to navigate all the rush-hour traffic. Trish had time to call.

"Hello?" Patsy's thin voice answered on the fourth ring.

"Hey, baby girl," Trish said. She'd always wondered why her mother had named two of her daughters after her—Trish and Patsy. They were all Patricia.

"Trisha!" Patsy squealed. "I miss you. When are you going to come back? Are you going to send me any more presents? I really liked the cool notebooks you sent me last time."

"Whoa, whoa—slow down, girl." Trish couldn't help but grin at her youngest sibling. The Hello Kitty notebooks had been on super clearance here because no one wanted them, but out on the rez? They were a prized possession. "Are you still going to school? I expect to see a good third-grade report card before any more presents show up."

Patsy sighed heavily and Trish was sure she could hear the accompanying eye roll. "Yes. I'm going every single day. Mrs. Iron Horse says I'm her best reader."

"Good."

"When are you coming back?"

"Not for another couple of months," Trish replied gently.

"What? Why not?" Patsy pouted. "I thought you were going to come back after you finished your school."

"Something came up. I got a new job and I have to stay here for a while."

Patsy was silent as she thought this over. "Do you like it? The new job?"

"Yes," Trish said without hesitating. The good food, the nice house, the amazing view—even without the huge paycheck, this was something of a dream job. That didn't even count Nate Longmire. And Nate? He counted for quite a lot. "I'll be home after the job is over. Is Mom home?"

"No, she got a new job, too. But Dad's here—you want to talk to him?"

"Sure. Put Tim on." As far as Patsy was concerned, Tim was her father. He'd come into their lives when Patsy had been only two. But Trish couldn't think of Tim as her father. He was a good guy, but she just couldn't do it.

"Daddy!" Patsy yelled in Trish's ear. She jerked the phone away from her head and winced. For such a little girl, Patsy had a heck of a set of lungs. "It's Trish!" Then she said in a normal voice, "I hope you can come home this summer. Then I can show you the award I got for writing an essay in Lakota!"

Homesickness hit Trish hard. She'd been there for all the other kids' awards and honors. She'd spent her entire adolescence making sure that the other kids got to basketball practice or assemblies or awards ceremonies. But she'd missed the past five years of that. "That's *so* awesome, baby girl. I can't wait to see it."

"Here's Daddy. Bye, Trish!"

"Bye, Patsy."

"Hey, Trish," Tim said in his gruff voice.

"Hi, Tim. How's it going?"

"Not bad. Your mom got a new job. Your sister Millie

got her a job at the state trooper's office. She's typing up the police reports at night."

"Really? Does she like it?" Because the Pat that Trish remembered couldn't hold down anything—a man, a job, a house. Nothing. It'd all been on Trish.

"Eh," Tim said. "You know how she is. But she gets to find out a lot of gossip as it's happening and she likes that, so I think she'll stay with this for a while."

"Yeah," Trish said. "I know how she is. Hey, the reason I'm calling is that I got a new job and I wanted to give you the address I'll be at for the next month."

"Gimme a sec," Tim said. She heard him rustling through papers and pens. "Okay, shoot."

Trish recited the address and then the new phone number. "I got a huge signing bonus," she went on. "I can pay you back that $350 you loaned me for my security deposit."

There was a moment of silence on the line that Trish wasn't sure how to interpret. "Trish, that was a gift."

"Well, I can pay you back. This is a really good job and—"

"Trish." It was as sharp as she'd ever heard Tim speak. "It was a gift. I've tried to help out all your brothers and sisters here, but you were so independent. The best I could do for you was to front you a little traveling money and give you a chance."

"You really don't have to do that," Trish said. Her throat was in danger of closing up and she wasn't sure why. "I mean, if you hadn't come along, I wouldn't have been able to leave. I'd have had to stay home and..." and continue being a mother to Pat's babies.

Trish never would have made it to San Francisco, never would have gotten one degree and almost completed a second one—never would have started her charity. She'd be stuck on that rez, no prospects and no hope. Nothing but doing her best to make sure that all of her siblings had the best chance *she* could give *them*.

"You don't have to give me anything more than what you've already given me," she finished in a low whisper, her voice shaking. "At least use it to get the kids something."

Tim had the nerve to laugh. "You always were the hardest of hard-headed kids. Toughest girl I ever did meet. I guess you had to be, what with Pat being Pat."

Then, before she quite realized it, she asked, "Why do you stay with her?"

She'd always wanted to know. She got why men would hook up with Pat—she was beautiful and liked to have a good time. Despite the ten kids, she still had a good figure. But looks weren't everything and no one else had lasted anywhere near as long as Tim. Sooner or later, Pat's drama would cancel out whatever good grace her face bought her and men would walk. Sometimes that was a good thing and sometimes it wasn't.

Tim kind of chuckled. "Love does funny things to a man, I guess." He sounded wistful. "I know she's not perfect and I'm not, either. I got the failed marriages to prove it. But there's something about being with her that makes me feel right with the world. And when you've seen as much of the world as I have, you know that's no small thing."

"Yeah, I guess…"

Tim laughed. "You're an old soul, Trish. You had to grow up early and quick. But take it from an old man— you're still young. You'll know what I mean one of these days. Keep the $350 and do something nice for yourself or run it through your charity or whatever. It's your money. I don't want it back."

"Thank you, Tim. I…" She swallowed, trying to get her voice under control. "It means a lot to me."

"Don't mention it. You want me to tell your mom you called?"

"That'd be great. Tell her I'm glad she's liking her new job, too."

"Will do. Take care, Trish."

The call ended. Trish sat in the back of a very nice car being driven by a very nice man, taking her back to a very nice house with a home-cooked meal and an attractive, interesting billionaire who liked *her*.

There was nothing about this that made her feel right with the world.

Seven

He couldn't tie the tie. This was why he paid Stanley money—to tie his damn ties for him.

Every time Nate tried to loop the ends around and under, just like the how-to video on YouTube, it came out... not tie-like. More like a four-year-old's attempt to tie his shoes than a polished, James Bond–like piece of neckwear.

"Hell," he mumbled as he undid the mess again. Maybe he wouldn't wear the bow tie. Maybe he'd go tieless and proclaim it was the latest fashion trend. It might even be a fun sociological experiment—how many people would follow suit because the richest man in the room said so?

Or he could still just cancel. That was an option, too. Sure, it was a gala sponsored in part by the Longmire Foundation and yes, people were probably starting to wonder if he'd died, since he hadn't been seen in public in three weeks. But he was Nate Longmire. He could do whatever he wanted.

"Knock, knock," Trish said from the doorway. "We came to say good-night."

Nate turned and saw Trish silhouetted from the light in the hallway. Jane was in her arms, her little head tucked against Trish's neck.

Mental correction—he could do *almost* whatever he wanted.

"Ready for bed?" he asked.

Jane turned her head away from him, which Trish had explained meant not that she didn't like him, but that the little girl was too tired to process.

Still, it stung in an entirely childish way. Nate crossed the room and kissed the back of Jane's head. "Good night, Janie. Sleep well."

He straightened up. Trish was looking at him, her large brown eyes taking in everything.

They stood like this a lot—so close together he could see the way her eyes shifted from a lighter brown to a deeper chocolate color. Close enough to kiss, except for the baby in between them. And, of course, there was no kissing.

In theory, he was getting better at not thinking about it. It was a nice theory, too. But right now...

She blinked, which pulled him out of his thoughts and back into reality. "You need some help with your tie?"

"You know how to tie a tie?"

The corners of her mouth quirked up. "I can't do much worse, I suppose. Can you wait until Jane's down?"

"Sure." He watched as she turned and walked across the hall. She settled into the glider chair and told Jane a story about Goldilocks and the Three Bears while the baby had her bedtime bottle.

Nate knew he should stay in his room, finish getting ready, maybe try the tie one more time. That was the safe thing to do—the legally advisable thing to do. But he was drawn across the hall, watching Trish rock Jane to sleep.

There it was again—that feeling of absolute peace as he watched Trish nurture the baby. She looked up at him, her eyebrows raised as if she were expecting him to ask a question or something, but he just shrugged a shoulder and watched.

Yeah, it could be that the serenity was simply because he was so damned relieved that Jane was being well cared for—that he wasn't solely responsible for her tiny person. But there was something more to this, something he didn't quite recognize.

Something Stanley had said came back to him—"I've yet to see you actually talk to a woman like you talk to *her*."

Comfort? Familiarity? No, that wasn't quite it, either. They'd only been coexisting for the past week, really. They'd had some good chemistry at a coffee shop and then he'd hired her in a moment of true desperation.

Jane finished her bottle and Trish gently patted her back before laying her out in the crib. She touched her fingertips to her lips and then brushed them over Jane's head as she murmured, "Good night, sweetie."

Then she turned and, slowly, walked toward him. He knew he needed to move—at the very least, he needed to get out of the way so they could shut the door and let Jane sleep.

But as she approached him, a knowing smile tugging on the corners of her mouth, he couldn't move. She was beautiful, yes, but there was so much more to her than that. She was kind and thoughtful and, perhaps most importantly, she didn't make him feel like an idiot.

She didn't hesitate. She walked right up to him and took hold of the ends of his tie. "Here," she said in a breathy whisper, gently pushing him back and out of the doorway. His hands lifted themselves up and settled around her waist—for balance, he justified after the fact. "Let me."

Without releasing her grip on his tie, she turned and pulled Jane's door shut. Then they were moving again as she backed him toward his bedroom.

He let her. He'd let her do whatever the hell she wanted right now. If she wanted to tie his tie, that'd be fine. If she wanted to rip his shirt off his chest, well, that'd be fine, too. He had other tuxedo shirts.

"Ah," she breathed, stopping well short of the bed. *Damn*. "I think I can do this."

"I'm sure it'll be better than what I was coming up with."

She grinned as she started looping the tie. "You look good in a tux. Very…"

He stood a little straighter. Her body underneath his hands was so hot he was practically sweating. "Yes?"

"Very grown-up. Not like a Boy Billionaire at all." He felt the tie tightening around his neck.

"I suppose that's a good thing?" Was that the same as "incredibly attractive"? That's what she'd told him once, when he was having a very bad day.

"It is. Damn." The tie loosened. "Let me try again."

He grinned down at her. "I think that's the first cuss word I've heard you say."

"Is it? I guess I've trained myself not to say bad words around kids." The necktie tightened again. "Where are you going tonight?"

"The Opera House for the gala charity function for ARTification, a big fund-raiser. The Longmire Foundation is a sponsoring partner." Her eyebrows jumped. "Well, that just means I gave them money and didn't do any of the planning."

She grinned, but it faltered. "Okay, I think I know what to do this time." One of her fingers touched the underside of his chin and lifted. "Look up, please."

Her touch took his theoretical mastery of his desire for her and pretty much reset it at zero. It took all of his concentration not to dig the pads of his fingertips into her glorious hips.

"I wanted to take you to this," he said before he knew what he was doing.

Her hands stilled for a moment. "You did?"

"Yes."

"You didn't ask me."

"I didn't think you'd say yes." He was careful to keep his chin up. "I don't know if you know who Martin Finklestein is, but he's pretty much decided that I should marry his granddaughter."

"And that's a problem?"

"Lola Finklestein makes me nervous." He forced a small smile. "Don't tell anyone I said that."

She didn't respond as she adjusted the tie. He felt her hands smoothing the bow. The tips of her fingers fluttered over his neck, right above his collar. Blood began to pound in his ear. "Is that why you wanted me to go with you? To run interference with Lola?"

He should say yes. He should back away. He should do *anything* but look down at her, so close. So damn close and not a single baby in between them.

But then her hands were smoothing over the shoulders of his tuxedo shirt, running down the front of the shirt. *She* was touching *him*.

"No." His hands moved without his explicit permission, tightening around her waist and then sliding toward her back. Pulling her in. He wanted to fill his hands with her skin, to know how she'd feel under him. Or over him. He wasn't picky. "I wanted…"

He swallowed and looked down. She was staring up at him, her lips parted and her cheeks flushed. She looked… like a woman who wanted to be kissed. He didn't know if she stepped into him or if he stepped into her, but suddenly what space had existed between them was gone and her arms were around his neck and he was lifting her toward his lips.

"You," he whispered. And then her lips were against his and he was kissing her back and it was good. *So* good. His hands kept right on moving of their own accord, sliding down until he'd cupped her bottom, the pads of his fingertips digging in as he pushed her higher. Her mouth opened for him and he tasted her, dipping his tongue into her honeyed sweetness. He went hard in an instant, pressing against the soft warmth of her stomach. Her nipples seemed to respond, growing hard and hot against his chest—so hot he could feel them through his shirt.

God, her mouth—this kiss—it was right. She was *right*, tucked in his arms where he could taste her and feel her body pressed against his and—and—

She pulled away. Not very far, but far enough that he had to stop kissing her, which was harder to do than he expected.

Her arms unlinked from around his neck and then, as coolly as if the kiss had never happened, she was smoothing the shirt over his shoulders. "You're going to be late."

"Um…yeah." That was not exactly the kind of thing a man liked to hear after the kind of kiss that left said man practically unable to walk. "I should—I should go."

She stepped away from him and it was only then that he saw how the kiss had affected her. Her eyes were glazed and her chest was heaving with what he hoped was desire. As he watched, the tip of her tongue darted out and ran over her top lip as if she were tasting his kiss and he almost lost it. Almost fell to his knees to beg her forgiveness but he was *going* to sleep with her, contractual language be damned. All that mattered was him and her and absolutely no bow ties.

She took another step back. "Don't—" She took a deep breath, which did some interesting things to her chest. "Don't let Lola steamroll you, okay?"

He managed a perfectly serviceable grin, as if her body in his arms was not a big deal at all. "Don't worry. I won't."

Nate didn't want to do this. He did not want to walk into one of the premiere high-society events of the social

season. He did not want women to look at him like he was
a lamb being led to sacrifice on the altar of Eligible Billionaire Bachelors. He didn't want to sit through a dinner
on a dais in front of the room and know that people were
watching him to see if he would do something of note.

"Mr. Longmire," an older gentleman who looked
vaguely familiar said as he hurried forth and shook Nate's
hand vigorously. "We weren't sure if you were actually
going to make it."

"Yes," Nate said, feeling the wall go up between him
and his surroundings. He hated social events in general
and formal ones in particular. The only way to get through
this was to pretend that he was somehow above the pro-
ceedings. That's how he'd gotten through the lawsuits and
it probably had contributed to his reputation as being ruthless.

He'd be much happier back home—even if Trish had
locked herself in her room and he spent the night in the
media room, staring at code.

He'd kissed her.

At the very least, he'd kissed her back.

But hot on the heels of that delicious memory of her
tasting him and him tasting her, a terrible thought occurred to him.

He'd broken the deal.

Oh, *no*. How could he have done that? A deal was a deal
and he *always* kept a deal.

Except for this. Except for Trish.

Worst-case scenarios—each more terrible than the
last—flipped through his mind. They all ended in basically the same way—Trish packing up her things and being
gone by morning, all because he couldn't resist her.

The older gentleman's welcoming smile faltered. "Yes,
well, this way, please. Mr. Martin Finklestein has been
asking after you."

"I bet he has." The older man's smile faltered so much that he lost his grip on it entirely, which made Nate feel bad. He was sure the rumor mill was working overtime as it was. "Lead on, please."

The older man—Nate could *not* remember his name—turned and all but scurried off toward the bar. Alcohol was already flowing, all the better to get people to crack open their wallets.

Nate followed. He was aware of people pausing in their conversations and watching him as he passed, but he was too worried about what Trish might be doing at this very moment to give a damn.

"Ah, Nate." The bright—some might say grating—voice of Lola Finklestein snaked through the hushed conversations and assaulted his ears. "There you are!"

He turned toward the voice. It was a shame, really. Her voice notwithstanding, Lola was a beautiful woman. She had a mass of thick black curls that were always artfully arranged. She had a swan's graceful neck and a slim figure. She was a beloved patron of the arts and of course she was heiress to the Finklestein fortune. By all objective measures, she was one hell of a catch.

Despite it all, Nate couldn't stand her. Her voice rubbed his nerve endings raw and she always had an odd scent, like…peaches and onions. He couldn't imagine spending the rest of his life stuffing cotton balls in his ears and lighting scented candles to cover the smell of her perfume.

Especially not after that kiss. Not after having Trish in his arms.

"Here I am," he agreed, feeling like a condemned man standing before the gallows.

"We've been worried sick about you. Where on earth have you been keeping yourself for the last three weeks? You know that the Celebration of the Zoo last week was just no fun without you."

"Couldn't be helped," Nate said. Which was a lame excuse—but still much better than being subjected to all kinds of condolences from this crowd. That was one of the reasons he kept Brad and Elena's deaths out of the press. He simply couldn't bear the thought of Lola hugging him and crying for his family.

He kept his back straight and what he hoped was a polite smile on his face. Of course, he'd seen photos of his "polite smile." It barely broke the threshold of "impolite snarl," but it was the best he could do.

He just wanted to be back at home. With Trish.

Was there a chance, however small, that the kiss had been the start of something else? Something more?

"Well, you're here now," Lola said, leaning in to brush kisses across both of his cheeks. "Oh, I have someone I want you to meet." She turned. "Diana?"

The name barely had a moment to register before a blonde woman in a blue dress separated from the others. Nate's brain crashed so fast, it felt like someone had tripped the surge protector in his mind.

She looked different now. Her face was tighter, her breasts larger—and was her nose slimmer, too?

Diana *Carter.*

The woman who'd nearly ruined him.

"Oh," she said in the breathy voice that he'd only heard on a few occasions—like when he'd told her about the first big round of investing he'd managed to secure for SnAppShot. And when he'd introduced her to Brad. "Nate and I do know each other. We go way back."

"Diana. You're looking…lovely." He realized he'd forgotten his polite smile, but this was possibly the worst thing that could have happened tonight.

Well, not the worst. Trish could have slapped him after that kiss. She could still leave.

But this was a close second.

Diana batted her eyes at him.

Damn it all. A *very* close second.

"I need to talk to you. Privately," he added as Lola stepped forward. Lola frowned.

Diana's demure face froze before she purred, "Of course."

"This way." Nate stalked off to a corner, chasing a lingering waiter away with a glare. "What are you doing here?" he demanded when they could speak without being overheard.

She gave him a reproachful look, as if he'd wounded her pride. "Is that any way to greet your fiancée?"

His teeth ground together. "*Former* fiancée. And yes, it is."

"About that." She sighed, her new and improved chest rising dramatically. "I was actually hoping to talk to you."

Nate's mouth opened to tell her where she could go but he slammed the brakes on and got his mouth shut just in time. If he looked hard enough, he could see the woman he'd once thought he'd loved. The Diana he'd known had been pretty enough, but with glasses and a habit of smiling nervously. She'd been shy and a little geeky and intelligent—exactly the kind of woman he'd thought he'd needed.

Until he'd taken her home to meet his family. And then she'd revealed that she was something more than all that.

"Why?"

Diana dropped her gaze and then looked up at him through her thick lashes. It felt entirely calculated. "I thought...we could let bygones be bygones." She exhaled through slightly parted lips. "I thought we might start over."

His mental circuitry overloaded and suddenly he was back at a single blinking cursor on an otherwise blank screen. The woman who'd broken his heart *and* tried to claim half of his company as her own because they'd just started dating when Nate thought it up— "You want to *start over*?"

She had the nerve to look hopeful. "Yes."

No. *No.*

"Brad's dead."

This time, Diana's reaction wasn't schooled or calculated. The blood drained out of her face and she took a shocked step backwards. "What?"

"You remember Brad? My older brother, the one you slept with because—and stop me if I'm not remembering this part correctly—you told me it was because he was 'like me' but better? He's dead."

Diana fell back another step. Her hand dropped to her side and what was left of her champagne spilled onto the floor. "What—when?"

"After we settled in court, he married an old girlfriend and they had a baby. They were very happy." He didn't know why he was telling her this. Only that, on some level, he felt like she deserved to know. "Until three weeks ago. A car accident. And now they're both dead."

Diana covered her mouth with her hands, her eyes painfully wide. "I didn't—I hadn't heard. I didn't know."

"No, of course not. After you cheated on me—after you tried to cheat me out of my company—I learned to keep things close to the vest. I learned how to avoid giving people anything they might use against me. I learned how to keep things out of the media."

Diana shook her head from side to side, as if she could deny that she'd changed him. That he'd let her change him. She took another step back and Nate matched it with a step forward. "I have you to thank for that. So, to answer your question, no. We can't start over. We can't go back. I can't trust you. Not now, not ever. You said it yourself, didn't you? 'I can do better.' That's the justification you had for falling into Brad's bed. He was better than me in everything but brains. That's the justification you used to try and take half of SnAppShot. And now that I'm the richest damn man in the room, you realize you can't do better, can you?"

"No—that's—I'm—"

He couldn't stop. He couldn't lock it down and bury all of this behind his wall of distance. In a moment of panic, he even tried to recall the original code to give him some measure of control over himself, but all he had was a flash of white-hot anger. Because she'd changed him. She'd made him afraid to be himself because being Nate Longmire hadn't been good enough. And he was tired of only being good enough because he was a billionaire.

That's not how Trish saw him. He was not a bank account to be conquered. He was a man who hadn't figured out all the mechanics of changing a diaper, who wasn't afraid to ask for help. He was not a meal ticket to be exploited until there was nothing left.

"It is. And I'm not the same naive nerd anymore, grateful for a pretty girl who didn't think I was a total loser."

"I never said that about you." She seemed to be regaining her balance. "I *cared* for you."

"But you didn't care enough." All of his anger bled out of him.

She had changed him. She'd made him tougher, smarter. He knew how to play the game now. It wasn't all bad. Just a broken heart. Everyone had one, once. He couldn't hold a grudge. "I wish you luck, Diana. I hope you find the man who's good enough for you. But it's not me. It never was me and we both know it. Now, if you'll excuse me."

He turned and walked off, pushing through the crowd like they were just so many sheep in Armani tuxedos. He couldn't bear to be here for another moment. He needed to breathe again and he couldn't do that with this stupid tie around his neck.

"Nate? Wait!"

He didn't know why he slowed. He'd said what he needed to say. But he slowed, anyway.

Diana Carter—the woman who had held so much sway over his life—caught up to him. "Nate," she said, her perfectly made-up eyes wet with unshed tears. "I'm sorry. I'm sorry for what I did. I'm sorry about your brother and his wife. Please—" Her chest hiccupped a little. She reached over and touched his shoulder. "Please accept my condolences on your loss."

"Thank you." He patted her hand where she was touching him and then, on impulse, lifted her hand to his lips.

She nodded in acceptance. "She's a lucky woman."

"Who?"

Diana gave him a watery smile, then she leaned up on her toes and brushed a kiss on his cheek. "Whoever she is. Goodbye, Nate."

"Goodbye, Diana." Their hands touched for another moment and then, by unspoken agreement, they separated. Nate had to bail. He couldn't do this, he couldn't sit in the front of this crowded room and pretend he was above the dinner and the speeches and all the people trying to figure out how to get closer to him. He couldn't put up his walls. Hell, he couldn't find his walls. Even his original code, which always kept him calm, failed him.

"Nate?" The voice was unmistakable. *Lola.* "Nate! Where are you going? You just got here!" Honestly, it was like fingernails down a chalkboard.

Nate kept going. He'd had things to say to Diana. He'd been close to marrying her, after all. But Lola? No, he didn't have things to say to her.

He dug out his phone and called for a hired car as he stalked out of the Opera House.

He had things he wanted to say to Trish.

He hoped like hell she'd listen.

Eight

Trish had her laptop on her lap, her thesis document open. She wasn't looking at it.

She wasn't looking at anything, really. Her eyes were focused out the big curved picture window in Nate's front parlor, but the darkness was not what she was seeing.

No, what she was seeing was the way Nate's pulse had jumped in his throat when she'd grabbed the ends of his tie. She was feeling the way his hands had settled around her waist.

She was tasting the kiss on her lips. *His* kiss.

This was a fine how-do-you-do, wasn't it? She'd kissed him. She didn't kiss people. She didn't sleep with people. She kept anyone who might even be remotely interested in her at twenty paces. Technically, that made her a twenty-five-year-old virgin, although she'd never thought about it in those terms. Not often, anyway. Sure, sex was probably a lot of fun—why else did her mother keep having it?— but she wasn't going to pay for twenty minutes of pleasure with the rest of her life.

She was not her mother's daughter, damn it all. At least, she hadn't been until one week ago. She was only four months from being twenty-six. By the time Pat Hunter was twenty-six, she had three kids, was pregnant with her fourth and had six more yet to come. She couldn't hold a job or a man. She was barely getting by.

That's not what Trish was. Trish was educated. She had a plan. She had things to do, things that would be derailed by something so grand as falling in love and so base as getting laid. She kept her eyes on the prize and her pants firmly zipped.

Until Nate. Until the very moment when he'd walked out on stage, if she was going to be honest about it. She hadn't had a single intention of doing anything remotely sexual with, about, or to Nate Longmire when she'd researched him. She'd noted he was attractive in the same way she might admire a well-carved statue, but there'd been no attraction. No desire.

There sure as hell was now. Because she'd kissed him. Prim, proper—some would say prudish—Patricia Hunter had kissed Nate Longmire.

What was she doing?

Wondering what sex with Nate would be like, that's what. Wondering if she'd actually go through with it, or if her healthy respect for the consequences would slam her legs shut again.

She could do it, after all. She was smart enough to use protection. She could enjoy safe sex with a man she was attracted to without losing herself in him, like Pat always had.

Couldn't she?

Dimly, she was aware of traffic outside, but it wasn't until the front door slammed shut that she became aware of her surroundings.

Then he was there. Nate Longmire filled the parlor doorway, each hand on the door frame as if he was physically holding himself back.

"Nate! Is everything all right?" She glanced at the clock. It was only 8:45. "I wasn't expecting you home for hours."

"I want you to know something," he said, his voice low and from somewhere deep in the back of his throat.

A shiver raced down her back at his commanding tone. "I want you to understand—I do *not* break a deal."

He bit the words out as if he were furious with them—or with her. She sat there for moment in a state of shock. This was, by far and away, the most enraged she'd ever seen him. "Oh?"

"I keep my word. My word is my bond. That's how my father raised me." She saw his fingers flex around the doorjamb. Would he rip the wood right off the wall? "When I say I'm going to do something—or not do something—then that's how it is. Canceling those two events because of Brad and Elena—it drove me nuts. But it couldn't be helped."

She closed her laptop and set it aside. She couldn't tell if he was going to fire her for kissing him or rip her clothes off. And worse—she didn't know what she wanted to happen. "I see."

"It's when people break their word to me, that's when the trouble starts. People make promises to me and then they break them and I won't stand for it."

He spoke with such conviction. Surely he wasn't trying to sound erotic, but heat spiked through her. He was barely holding himself back. She should probably be afraid of this display of anger—of power.

She was *totally* turned on. "You can be ruthless. That's your reputation."

"I have to be." It came out anguished, as if it wounded him to sue people back to the Stone Age. "Kill or be killed." Even from twenty feet away, she could see the white-knuckled grip he had on the frame. But he didn't take another step into the room. "I was engaged. To be married."

"You were?"

"To Diana Carter." The admission seemed to hollow him out a bit.

The name rang a bell. Nate Longmire v. Diana Carter. The court case. The rumors that maybe there'd been something else between them, rumors that could be neither confirmed nor denied because the court records were sealed. "Wait. Isn't that the woman you sued over the right to the SnAppShot code?"

He nodded, a short crisp movement of his head that did nothing to dislodge his grip on the door frame. "She was there tonight. I try not to think about her, but I realized tonight that because of what she did, she's affected *everything* that I do."

This time, Trish stood. When she did—when she took a step toward him—his head jerked up and he got that ferocious look on his face again. "What did she do?"

"We were engaged. I took her home to meet my family and she slept with my brother."

Her mouth dropped open in surprise. Not what she was expecting to hear. "She broke her promise."

"And then claimed half the company was hers, since we'd been together when I started it."

"And tonight?" She took another step toward him. And another.

"She wanted to start over. But I can't trust her." He swallowed, his Adam's apple bobbing above his bow tie. "Not like I trust you."

She considered this. "Do you? I mean, we haven't known each other very long."

"I trust you with my niece's life. That's far more important than a stupid piece of code."

She took a few more steps toward him, closing the distance between them. His head snapped up. "Don't come any closer."

"Why not?"

"Because I keep my promises. And I promised you that I would not have sex with you. That I would not take advantage of you just because you're beautiful and intelligent and I'm as comfortable with you as I've ever been with any woman, including Diana. Just because I trust you." She took another step forward and he actually backed up. He didn't let go of the door frame, but his feet were now in the hall. "And if you come any closer, I'm not going to keep my promise."

The words ripped out of his chest and seemed to hit her in the dead center of hers. She put her hand over her heart to make sure it was still beating.

"All those women tonight, trying to catch my eye," he went on. "Lola and Diana and the rest of them, looking at me and seeing a prize they could win. And all I could see—all I could think about—was *you*. I wanted to take you because I wanted you there with me. And since that couldn't happen—since Jane is upstairs—I came home."

"Will you keep your promise to me?"

He swallowed again, looking haunted. "I *have* to. Three more weeks, right? I'll hire a new nanny and you'll move out and then…then I'll ask you to dinner. That's how it has to be. I can't kiss you. Not like I did earlier. Not like I wanted to since I met you. I gave you my word." He sounded like he was ripping his heart out with that last bit.

A promise. A promise he intended to keep, no matter how much it hurt him. She didn't know too many men who kept their promises like that. Hell, she didn't know too many women. People lied and cheated and did all sorts of horrible things to each other in the name of love all the time with very little thought to how it might affect others. Just like her mother had.

Just like her father had.

But not Nate. He'd given her his word and he'd keep it, even if it killed him.

That made all the difference in the world.

She didn't give him the chance to back away any farther. She closed the remaining distance between them so fast that he didn't have time to react. She stepped into him and put her arms around his neck and refused to let him go.

He tensed at her touch. "Don't." It was half order, half plea.

"Because you'll break your promise?"

He closed his eyes. He was back to his white-knuckle grip on the door frame, doing everything in his power to not touch her. "Yes."

She loosened her arms from around his neck and trailed her fingertips until she had the ends of her best bow tie in her hands. "I made no such promise, did I?"

Nate jolted against her—hard. She swore she heard the crack of wood giving way. "You don't sleep with people. You said so yourself."

She pulled on the ends of the tie, slowly loosening it until it hung down against his tuxedo shirt. "People in general, no." She slipped the top button free. He had a nice neck. The next button came loose.

"Trish," he groaned. His eyes were still closed but his head had started to tilt forward—toward her. "What are you doing?"

She undid another button. "Making sure you keep your promise."

His eyes flew open and he stared down at her in true shock. *"How?"*

"By seducing you." As the third button gave, she leaned up on her tiptoes and placed a kiss against the exposed skin of his neck, right under his Adam's apple. She could hear his pulse pounding through his veins. "If you want me to."

Then—and only then—did he relinquish his hold on the poor door frame. His arms swung down and surrounded her with his strength. She wanted to melt against him, but she didn't. Not yet. There'd be time for that later.

She toyed with the pointed tips of his collar. "Do you want me to?"

"This doesn't have anything to do with money or charities or anything, right?"

She leaned forward and kissed his neck again as she worked another button free. His pulse jumped under her lips, a wild beating that matched her own heart's rhythm. She was doing this, seducing Nate Longmire, the Boy Billionaire.

Except, she wasn't, not really. She wasn't seducing one of the most eligible Billionaire Bachelors. She was just seducing Nate. Beautiful, geeky Nate, who *always* kept his promises.

"No." Then she skimmed her teeth over his skin and felt him shudder. His body's response did things to her. Sweet, glorious heat flushed her breasts and spread farther. She was doing this to him. And he was letting her. "This is between you and me. That's all I want. Me and you."

"Trish," he groaned.

"I take that as a yes, then." She pushed him back, but only so far that she could slide his tuxedo jacket off his shoulders. It hit the ground with a whoosh and then she was working at his buttons again.

He didn't touch her, didn't try to lift her T-shirt over her head. He just stood there as she undid the rest of his buttons, his chest heaving with the effort of *not* touching her.

He had on a white undershirt, which was irritating. Formal clothing had so many layers. She slid her hands under his tuxedo shirt and stepped in again. This time, she kissed him proper.

And this time? He kissed her back. His arms folded around her again and she was pressed against his massive chest.

Oh, *yes*. Trish didn't actually know much about the art of seduction, but even she knew that was a good thing.

The heat focused in that spot between her legs and the only way she could think to ease the pressure was to lift one leg and wrap it around Nate.

But it didn't ease the pulsing heat. Instead, when Nate grabbed her under her thigh and lifted her higher, it brought her core in contact with something else—something long and thick and—

"Upstairs," she demanded, her back arching into that thick length.

She wasn't sure what she'd expected him to do. Turn and race up the stairs, maybe. That's what she would have done.

But she wasn't Nate. He hefted her up and leaned her back against the poor, misused door frame and kissed the hell out of her. She really had no choice but to put her legs around his waist, did she? And when she did, his erection ground against her. "Oh. *Oh!*"

"Mmm," he hummed against her mouth as he devoured her lips. Then he shifted his hips and heat exploded between them. Her body shimmied under his.

She could have stayed like that forever, except the door frame was exacting its revenge on her back. "Take me to bed, Nate. *Now.*"

"Yes, ma'am," he said.

And then Trish was floating through the air as Nate carried her up the stairs as if she weighed nothing, as if each step weren't driving his erection against her, as if she weren't on the verge of climaxing when he bit down on her shoulder.

Oh, yes.

Then they were in his room and he was kicking his door shut—quietly—and he'd laid her out on the bed. He started to strip off his shirt, but she sat up and said, "No, stop. That's my job."

His hand froze on his cuff links. "It is?"

"I'm doing the seducing around here," she replied,

pushing his hand away and undoing the offending cuff link herself. "That was the deal, right?"

"Absolutely," he agreed.

So Trish got to her knees on the bed and undid his other cuff so that she could push the very nice shirt off his shoulders and then strip the undershirt off him and then *finally* she could see the massive chest.

"You are built," she whispered as she ran her fingers over his muscles.

She skimmed her fingertips over his nipples and was rewarded with another low groan. His only other reaction was to clench his hands into fists, but he held them by his side. He didn't say anything. The last of his self-control, hanging by a thread.

He had a smattering of dark brown hairs in the space between two nicely defined pecs and a treasure trail that ended in the waistband of his pants. She followed it with her fingertips, then hooked her fingers into his waistband and pulled him into her so she could kiss him.

"Trish," he moaned into her mouth. "You're going to kill me."

She responded by running her hands over the huge bulge in his trousers. The heat pouring off him was electric. *He* was electric, setting her nerves on fire and threatening to overwhelm her. He shuddered under her touch.

"Oh, my, Nate," she whispered as she stroked his length through the fine wool of his trousers. He was built in *so* many ways. "Oh, *my.*"

"Please," he begged.

"You have condoms?"

"Yeah. Somewhere."

"Go get them. Right now." Because once those pants got unbuttoned, there'd be no stopping, no turning back.

She might be doing the wild and crazy thing of seducing Nate Longmire, but that didn't mean she wanted to get carried away. She wanted to enjoy this night, this time, with him without having to deal with the consequences.

He pulled away from her so fast she almost toppled off the bed. She caught herself and sat back on her heels, watching him. She hadn't spent much time in his room. She'd seen it only when she'd tied his now-crumpled tie. It was the whole side of the house, with the bathroom in the back. The room was done in cool grays and blues, with a more modern touch than her room.

And the bed itself? She had no idea how they'd gotten a California King into this house but they had. And she was going to make good use of such a large bed.

He checked a drawer in the bedside table, then went around to the other side. "Got them," he muttered.

He came back to where she was waiting and stood there, an unopened box of condoms in his hand, like he wasn't sure what should happen next.

"Okay?" she asked. She had him shirtless and he was definitely interested, but now that he'd had a moment to think, a hint of doubt had crept into his eyes.

"Yeah. Yes," he repeated with more force. He closed his eyes and took a deep breath. "It's just…been a while." Then he opened his eyes and cupped her face and kissed her, soft and sweet and full of promise. "You?"

"You could say that." He lifted an eyebrow, but she didn't elaborate. She had no room in her life for antiquated notions of virginity, anyway. She'd already raised nine kids—ten, if she counted Jane. Her virginity was completely irrelevant to the situation.

But she could tell he was trying to figure out the best way to ask that question, so she went back on the offensive. She pulled him down into another kiss as she let her hands move over all those muscles.

"Shoes," she murmured. "Take them off."

He kicked off his shoes and peeled off his socks, but

when he went for his waistband, she grabbed his hands. "Wait," she told him. "Watch."

Then, because it seemed like the thing to do, she stood on the bed. Slowly, she peeled her T-shirt over her head. Nate made a noise in the back of his throat that was part groan, part animalistic growl as he stared at her simple beige bra.

Then she undid the button and slid down the zipper on her jeans. As the jeans slipped past her hips, she wished she had a pretty matching set of underwear instead of ones of cheap cotton. She wanted to be sexier for him.

Not that he seemed to mind her mismatched set. As the jeans slid free of her legs and she kicked them off, his mouth fell open. "Trish," he groaned again, his arms held tight at his side, his hands fisted. "Look at you. You're *stunning*." His voice shook with raw desire.

And just like that, she felt desirable in spite of her under things. She walked over to where he stood. The added height of the bed meant that, instead of having to crane her neck up to look at him, she was a few inches taller than he was. She draped her arms around his neck again.

Stunning. She hadn't often felt beautiful. She'd had some people try to compliment her, but the best she usually got was "striking."

"And you, as I believe I noted before, are incredibly attractive."

He grinned up at her, the doubt gone from his eyes. "Can I touch you now or are you still seducing me?"

"I didn't say you couldn't touch me, did I?"

In response, his hands skimmed up the back of her thighs, over her bottom. He moved deliberately, trailing his fingertips along the waistband of her serviceable panties, over her hips, and along the elastic of her leg bands.

She couldn't help it. She closed her eyes and let her skin take in his every movement. She tingled under his touch, little shocks of pleasure wherever his fingertips caressed her.

"You are so beautiful, Trish," he whispered against her chest. Then he pressed his lips against the inner curve of her breast, right above the bra cup. "Let me show you how beautiful you are."

He turned his head and kissed the other breast as he began to unhook her bra. A moment of panic flashed over her—what was she doing? Having sex with Nate? Was she *crazy?*—but then the bra gave and he pulled it off her shoulders and she moved her arms to let it fall helplessly between them and he—and he—

He licked her left nipple like he was licking an ice cream cone. As his tongue worked her into a hard, stiff peak, he glanced up at her. "Watch me," he ordered and then he closed his lips around her nipple and sucked.

"Nate!" she exclaimed in a whisper at the sudden pressure. She wanted to cry out and scream his name, but she didn't want to wake the baby. She laced her hands through his hair. "Oh…"

"Good?" he asked, his voice muffled against her skin.

"Yes," she said. In response, he sucked again, harder. *"Oh…"* she managed to say again. Her legs started to shake.

One of his hands slid down her back again, tracing her bottom before coming between her legs from behind. The position locked her body to his. Softly—so softly—his fingertips rubbed over the thin fabric of her panties. The sensation of someone that wasn't her touching her there was so overwhelming that she couldn't even make a noise.

"Open your legs for me," he whispered. "Let me show you how beautiful you are."

Despite the way he had her legs pinned with his arm, she managed to scoot her knees a little farther apart without losing her balance.

"Mmm," Nate hummed as he licked her other nipple. His fingers rubbed in longer strokes, so close to hitting that hot, heavy weight in the front.

So close—but not quite. He was going to drive her mad with lust. Her! Trish Hunter, who had always been above such base things. With Nate's mouth on her, his fingers against her—

She ground against his fingers as she held his head to her breast. "Nate," she moaned when his teeth scraped over her nipple. "Oh, *Nate...*"

"Like that. Just like that, Trish." His voice was low and deep and sent a shiver up her back. "Oh, babe."

She wasn't doing the seducing anymore. He'd taken the reins from her and she was only too happy to hand them over. She really didn't know what she was doing, after all. But Nate?

He knew. He knew *exactly* what he was doing to her.

Then his mouth left her nipples and he kissed his way down her stomach. He hooked his thumbs into the waistband of her panties and slid them down. And then she was nude before him, nothing between them but a pair of tuxedo pants.

She had a moment of panic—she hadn't exactly prepped for this encounter. As Nate drifted south and she lost her grip on his hair, she fought the urge to cover herself.

"Let me see you—all of you," Nate said, catching her hands and lifting them away. "You're so beautiful, Trish."

"Nate..." Now that he wasn't holding her up, her knees were practically knocking.

But that was as far as she got before he pressed a kiss against the top of her thigh, then the other. And then?

Then he gripped her by the hips, tilting her back ever-so-gently, and ran his tongue over the little button that he hadn't quite managed to hit earlier.

Her body seized up with pleasure. She'd touched herself, of course. But this? This was something else. Something entirely different.

"I—I can't stand," she gasped as his tongue stroked her again and again. Light heat shimmered along her limbs, making her muscles tighten and weaken at the same time. *So different*, she thought. "I can't take it, Nate."

He looked up at her and for the first time, she saw something wicked in his eyes. "Babe, we're only just getting started."

Nine

This was really happening. Nate wondered if he might be dreaming, but then he'd tasted her sweetness on his tongue. None of his dreams had been this good.

Trish, in the bare flesh, was so much better than any fantasy he'd had.

Her eyes went wide at his words. "What?"

If he were a suave kind of guy, he'd figure out how to sweep her off her feet and lay her out on the bed without causing bodily harm to either of them, but he wasn't going to risk that right now. So he took her by the hands and guided her down to her knees on the bed, which meant that they were almost eye-to-eye.

"When I'm done with you, you *won't* be able to stand," he promised, tilting her back in the bed. The look of shock on her face told him pretty much everything he needed to know.

She didn't have a whole lot of experience. Maybe none. And yet, she'd still worked him into a lather.

It was time to return the favor.

He hooked his elbows under her knees and pulled her to him. She made a little squeaking sound, so he said, "Let me love on you, Trish." Then he lowered his mouth to her again.

She really did have a honeyed sweetness to her and he couldn't get enough of it—of her.

Years of sexual frustration—of avoiding hookups and dodging would-be brides, all because he didn't want anyone to break a promise they never intended to keep— seemed to surge up within his chest and he poured all of that energy into every action of his mouth, his tongue, his teeth. Trish's hips shifted from side to side as he worked on her and her hands found their way back to his hair again.

"That's it, babe. Show me how you want it."

"We can't wake the baby," she panted in a forced whisper.

"I'll be quiet, I promise." Then he slipped a finger inside of her.

Her tight muscles clamped around him with such force that he almost lost it right then. He licked her again and was rewarded with a noise that went past a groan into almost a howl.

"Come for me, Trish. Show me what you can do." He flicked his tongue back and forth over her, so hard and hot for his touch.

"Nate," she gasped out. "Nate—oh, Nate!"

His name on her lips, his body inside of hers—this was worth it. Years of self-denial—all worth the way they fit together.

He reached up to grasp her dark pink nipple between his thumb and forefinger and pulled. Not hard, but enough that she gasped again and came up off the bed a couple of inches.

Then he felt it—her inner muscles clamped down on him and her head thrashed from side to side and her mouth opened, but nothing came out. She came silently, her gaze locked onto his.

He couldn't remember being this excited. He was probably going to lose it the moment he plunged into her wet heat, but it didn't matter. He'd done this for her, given her this climax.

But he couldn't waste time patting himself on the back. Trish propped herself up on her elbows, her eyes glazed with satisfaction. "Boy," she said weakly. "I'm sure glad I did the seducing here."

"Me, too." He forced himself to pull away from her. He needed to be rid of his pants right now. He was so hard he was going to break the damned zipper. That's what she did to him.

But she sat up and swatted his hands away from his trousers. "Mine," she said as she jerked the button free and ripped the zipper down. "I can return the favor." The pants fell down and there he was, straining his boxer-briefs to the point of failure. She ran her hands over his length again. "If you want."

There it was again—that hint of innocence. "I consider myself well and truly seduced." As he said it, she rubbed her thumb over his tip.

He jerked under her hands, so close already. He couldn't withstand the pressure of her mouth on him and he didn't want to disappoint her.

"Condoms," he got out through gritted teeth.

She snagged the box and haphazardly tore it open. He took a condom from her and held as still as he could while she yanked his underwear down.

He ripped open the foil packet but before he could sheath himself, she'd taken him back in hand. *"Built,"* she murmured, encircling his width with her hand and stroking up, then back down.

"Trish," he hissed. "I need to be inside you. *Right now.*"

She looked up at him with big eyes. She was panting now, the haze of desire edging back. "I love it when you're all ruthless like that."

He paused halfway through rolling on the condom, then finished the task at hand. "You do?"

"Very powerful." Her gaze darted down to where he was sheathed. "That'll...that'll work, right?"

"Right." He climbed onto the bed, scooting her back so that she was against the pillows as he went. "Tell me if it's not working, okay?"

"Okay," she said as she looped her legs around his waist.

He kissed her as he fit himself against her. "Beautiful," he murmured as he tried a preliminary thrust.

Her body took him in, but she still sucked in air.

"Okay?"

"I think—just a second—"

"Take your time. I've got all night." Which was not, in the strict sense of the word, true. He could feel her hips shifting beneath his as she adjusted to his width and it about killed him.

Then she shifted again, her hips rising toward him and, without being conscious of the motion, he pushed in deeper. "Oh!" she said, but he didn't hear any pain in her voice. Just surprise.

"Okay?"

"Yes. I think so..." Her hips flexed and her tightness eased back just enough that he was able to go deeper. And deeper. Until finally he was fully joined to her.

"Oh, babe," he groaned as he pushed back against the climax that already threatened to swamp him. "You feel so *good*."

"Um...okay."

He kissed her eyelids. Yeah, she'd never done this before. He had to make this count. "Ready?"

She looked worried, as if she were expecting a marching band to show up. "For?"

"This, babe." He withdrew and thrust back in, focusing on keeping his breath even and his climax firmly under control. *"This."*

"Oh. *Oh!*" As he pulled out and thrust in again, everything about her changed. Her hips rose up to meet him and her eyelids drifted shut as she felt him move inside of her. "Oh, *Nate*."

"Yeah, babe." They fell into a good rhythm, the give-and-take between his body and hers something different than he remembered. He wasn't as experienced as some, but he'd learned a lot during the two years he and Diana had been together.

He put that experience to good use now. He and Trish—they fit. Her warmth, wet and tight, took everything he had and then some, until she was arching her back and thrashing her head around and opening her mouth but not making a single noise as everything about her tightened down on him.

"So beautiful," he managed to get out again as her shockwaves pushed him faster and harder until he gave up the fight with himself and surrendered to her.

Then they lay still. He remembered to pull out so he didn't compromise the condom. But after that, he just lay on her chest.

"Oh, my," she finally breathed as she stroked his head.

"Is that a good 'oh, my' or a bad one?"

"Good. Very good." She sighed dreamily. "I didn't..." the words trailed off and she looked worried again.

He hefted himself up onto his forearms so he could look at her. "Thank you."

A wary look clouded her eyes. "For?"

He grinned down at her. "For not making me break my promise. Not at first, anyway."

"Oh." She exhaled. "I thought you were going to say something foolish, like thanking me for my virginity or something archaic like that."

He started to laugh in spite of himself. *Must be the euphoric high*, he thought, because he did not remember being this happy after sex. "Archaic?" He slid off to her side, but he didn't let go of her. One hand around her waist, pinning him to her chest. "You really hadn't done that before?"

After a moment where her body tensed up, she relaxed in his arms. "I didn't want to. I mean, I did, but..."

"You weren't ready to be a mother." That's what she'd said. He just hadn't realized how deeply that commitment went.

"No." She laced her fingers with his. "I didn't know it was going to be like that."

As the words trailed off, the keening wail of Jane crying cut across the hallway. "Oh," Trish said, visibly shaking off the last of her desire. She sat up and looked around as if coming out of a dream. "I've got to go."

He sat up and reached for her. "Trish—"

But she was out of bed, gathering up her clothes and all but sprinting out of his room. "I've got her," she called back over her shoulder, right before she pulled the door shut.

What had just happened here? One moment, she was sated and happy in his arms and the next?

Basically running away from him.

A sinking pit of worry began to form in his stomach. He tried to push it aside—she'd seduced him, not the other way around—but it didn't work. They might have followed the letter of their agreement, but not the real spirit of it.

He'd slept with her.

What had he done?

Trish used the bathroom and dressed quickly, making soothing noises to Jane the whole time.

She'd slept with Nate. Her first.

She needed to get Jane quieted back down so that Nate would go to sleep because she couldn't bear to talk to him right now, couldn't bear to lay in his arms and feel his body pressed against hers.

"Shh, shh, I'm here, sweetie," she hummed to Jane as she picked up the baby. She glanced at the clock. The little girl was up two hours before she should be. "Is it your teeth? Poor baby." For once in her life, she hoped it really was Jane's teeth—and not that Trish and Nate had been too loud.

She carried the baby downstairs and got one of the wet washcloths she'd stashed in the freezer. "Let's try this and see if we can go back to sleep, okay?" She headed back up to the nursery and sat in the glider, rocking Jane and humming softly as the little girl soothed her sore gums.

Trish wished she could soothe herself, but alas that didn't look like it was going to happen anytime soon. She kept a close eye on the door to the nursery, wanting Nate's shirtless form to appear and hoping like hell it didn't.

She'd slept with him. There was nothing wrong with that, per se. But…

She'd liked it. His mouth on her body, his body inside of hers? The way he'd made her feel?

God, how she'd liked it.

In the moment when he'd pulled free of her, she'd almost cried out to lose that connection with him. And when he'd tucked her against his chest, his arms tight around her waist?

She'd been on the verge of taking him in her hand—on the verge of seducing him a second time, just because she wanted that connection back. Because she wanted that feeling of clarity when his body pushed hers over the edge.

And she knew that, if he appeared in the doorway and said, "Come back to bed, Trish," she'd be helpless to say no, helpless to do anything but march right back into his bedroom and strip off her clothing again and explore his body over and over until they were both spent and dazed and the only thing in the world was Nate and Trish and a very big bed.

She would be his. Body, mind and soul. There'd be no turning back.

She'd be just like her mother.

This realization made her start, which jolted poor Jane. The baby started to fuss again. "Shh, shh," Trish whispered, finding a still-cold corner of the washcloth for Jane to chew on.

Of course Trish knew that sex had to be fun. That's why people did it so much, right? That's why her mother couldn't stay single—why she'd pick up a man at a bar and screw him in the parking lot and then, when he turned out to be an asshole, she couldn't kick him out of her life.

Trish had asked her once why she kept going with men who didn't even seem to like her. And Pat had replied with tears in her eyes, "Oh, Trish, honey, I know that the bad times can seem pretty bad. But when it's good…" and she'd gotten this far-away look in her eyes, a satisfied smile curling her lip up. "When it's good, it's *so* good."

Which hadn't made any sense to Trish at the ripe old age of ten because, as far as she could tell, there was nothing good about the men her mother picked.

As she'd grown up and come to understand the mechanics of sex—and as she'd explored her own body—she still hadn't understood what the big deal was. She could bring herself to a quick, quiet little orgasm, but that wasn't enough to make her want to throw away everything she'd worked for.

Except now she knew. She knew how a man could make her feel, make her body do things that Trish couldn't do to herself. Oh, Nate…with his big hands and bigger muscles and his damned principles about keeping his promises.

Jane had fallen asleep at some point in the past twenty minutes, but Trish was in no hurry to put the baby back in her crib. She needed this small child—needed the physical barrier Jane provided. Hadn't that been the problem tonight? Trish had tied Nate's tie without a baby between them and she'd kissed him because a man had no business looking as handsome as he did in that tux.

And then he'd come home early just because he wanted to see her. Her! She was nothing—a poor Indian woman who didn't even know who her father was. Tonight, Nate had walked away from heiresses and self-made women— women who matched his social standing and his love of modern technology—for her. There was no way she could keep up with him.

What a mess. Easily the biggest mess she'd ever gotten herself into, all because she liked him. Because she *let* herself like him instead of holding him at an arm's length.

What could she do? Quit? She looked down at the baby sleeping in her arms. She'd gotten Jane calmed down and mostly on a schedule. It'd be easier for Nate to hire a nanny now because he knew what to expect from a nanny and he knew what Jane needed.

But. Of course there was a "but."

If she quit, would he withhold the funding he'd promised? He'd signed a contract; so had she. She didn't think he would. He was a decent man—possibly the best man she'd ever met. But rejection did nasty things to people. She'd watched her mother curse and cry and throw their few dishes against the wall when she'd found out her current man was seeing someone on the side and Trish had huddled in her room with her siblings when the breakups happened.

But if Trish stayed…she'd want Nate again. And again. She'd want to spend the night trying different positions, different ways to make him cry out her name in that hoarse voice. She'd want to sleep in his bed, his strong arms firmly around her waist, his chest warming her back. She'd want to wake up with him and have breakfast with him out on the patio of this house and count the hours until

Jane went down for her nap so that Trish could pull Nate into his room and do it all over again.

She could stay here with him, raise his niece for him. She could do whatever he wanted, as long as he kept making love to her.

The intensity of this need scared her. For once in her life, she understood her mother, how she could overlook the health and safety of her children in favor of a man who might make her feel like Nate had made Trish feel.

Because if she stayed here with Nate and raised Jane—became a permanent nanny during the day and his lover at night—well, then what would happen to One Child, One World?

How was Trish supposed to look her baby sister in the eyes and say, "Yes, I know I said you should put your education and career ahead of any man, but he's a *really* great guy!"

Because that's what her mother would say. That's what her mother would do.

Trish was *not* her mother.

And that was final.

Ten

Nate drifted in and out of consciousness as he waited for Trish to come back. He heard her go downstairs and then, sometime later, he heard her go down again, which didn't make any sense. When had she come back up?

His head was heavy with sleep. He'd sort of forgotten how much really awesome sex took out of him. But when he heard her come back upstairs again and yet she still didn't come back into his room, he forced himself to roll over and check the time on his phone.

Three-thirty.

He blinked at the red numbers again, but they didn't change. That wasn't right, was it? She'd left the first time around eleven and he knew she hadn't come back to him.

He sat up and rubbed his eyes. Where was she? He hadn't heard Jane crying.

He slipped his briefs back on and silently opened his door. Both Jane's door and Trish's were shut.

Maybe she'd fallen asleep in the glider, he reasoned. Both she and the baby had passed out and that's why she hadn't come back.

He tiptoed across the hall and opened Jane's door. The glider was empty and the little girl was in her crib, making those noises that Trish had promised him were perfectly normal for babies to make.

Which meant only one thing. Trish had gone to bed. Alone.

He backed out of the nursery and closed the door. Then he looked at Trish's door. He could knock but the hint was not-so-subtle. She'd gone back to her own room instead of his.

He ran through the evening's events. He hadn't cornered her, hadn't pressured her. She'd come to him of her own accord. She'd started it—he'd finished it, though.

Foreplay? *Check*. Orgasms? *Double check*. Cuddling? A little, right until the baby cried. All good things—unless...

Unless she'd changed her mind—about him, about sex, about sex with him.

Well, he wasn't going to figure out this puzzle standing in the hallway in nothing but a pair of shorts in the middle of the night.

But tomorrow, he and Trish were going to talk.

Trish heard Nate's door open, heard Jane's door open. Oh, God—he was looking for her. Would he come to her door, begging her to come back to his bed?

She curled herself around her pillow, willing him not to. She had to be stronger than this. She had to hold herself back from him and that was going to be damnably hard at—she checked the clock—three thirty-seven in the morning.

Go back to bed, she mentally screamed into the night. *Don't come in here.*

Jane's door whispered shut. Trish heard Nate take a footstep toward her room, then another. She tensed with fear—or need. Her brain was shouting, *no!* while her body, her traitorous body, was already clamoring for his touch. Trish was this close to throwing the covers off and flinging open her door and rushing into his arms.

She had to be stronger. She *was* stronger, by God.

The footsteps stopped. The house was silent. She pictured Nate standing on the other side of her bedroom door—so close, yet so very far away.

Then, just when she couldn't stand it another second—she *had* to go to him—she heard him walking again. His footsteps grew more distant, and then his door shut.

She should have been relieved.

Why did she feel like crying?

Trish felt like hell. She supposed that was to be expected. Her body was punishing her for her late-night activities in ways that made regular old sleep deprivation look like a cakewalk.

Somehow, Trish got the bottle made and the coffee started. She didn't even bother to attempt breakfast. Her stomach was so nervous at the thought of Nate coming downstairs and—well, even looking at her would be bad enough. Talking would be sheer torture. Yeah, there was no way she could handle breakfast at this point.

The morning was hazy with fog, but Trish decided to sit out on the patio with Jane, anyway. Fresh air and all that.

Plus, it put a little more space between her and Nate. And maybe she could come up with a way to *not* throw everything she'd ever worked for away because of him.

Jane was fussy, which helped. Trish focused on the girl with everything she had. Jane was why Trish was here. Jane was why she needed to stay. Not because of Nate.

She really did need to finish the month, she thought as she held Jane's bottle for her. For one thing, the poor girl had been through a lot and was just getting settled into her routine. It would be another setback for her if Trish just up and left.

And for another, there was the money. The other reason she was doing this. Nate was going to fund One Child,

One World for the foreseeable future. She could not tuck tail and run just because she could fall in love with him.

She could *not* fall in love with him.

The idea was so crazy that she started laughing. Would it be possible to *not* fall for him? That was where her mother always screwed up. If she'd just wanted the sex, that would have been one thing. The trouble came when she fell in love with whatever man she had and refused to let him go, no matter what common sense dictated.

Maybe Trish could take the sex and leave the love. After all, she'd spent the past few decades not allowing herself to get close to anyone. And, up until the moment she met Nate, she'd been very good at it.

She could enjoy Nate, safely, and not love him. She could refuse to give into the madness that had ruled her mother. It would be—well, it'd be physical. Short-term and very physical. But nothing more.

Could she *do* that?

Behind her, she heard him in the kitchen. Unconsciously, she tensed, which made Jane pop off her bottle and start to whimper. "Oh, now," she soothed, getting Jane to take her bottle again. "None of that. That's my good girl."

Pots and pans rattled. He was making breakfast. He was just too damn nice, that was the problem. Too damn perfect. This would be so much easier if he'd been a royal ass, or a really lousy lover or just a horrible person all the way around. Was that too much to ask, for him to be awful? Because that was the kind of man who didn't interest her at all. That was the kind of man she'd never tumble into bed with.

How was she supposed to even *look* at him this morning? After what she'd done to him? And especially after what he'd done to her?

This was the awkward part of being a twenty-five-year-old virgin. Everyone else in the world had figured out how to handle the post-hookup interactions back in college. They either left afterward or slipped out of bed in the morning or…or she didn't know what. They probably never had to sit around, playing with a baby while their lovers made them breakfast.

Life was so much easier without sex in it.

But what could she do? Nothing. It's not like she could wander off into the fog with a baby in her arms to avoid talking to him. She had to sit here and deal with this like a grown-up, because that's what she was.

Finally, after what felt like a small eternity, she heard the patio door slide open and felt Nate walk out. "Good morning," he said as he set his coffee cup on the table. No tray—no breakfast.

"Hi," she got out. It sounded weaker than she wanted it to, damn it all.

He leaned over and kissed Jane's head, then turned and made eye contact with her. He held it for just a beat too long and panic flared up in her stomach. Was he going to kiss her? Yell at her? What was happening here?

Then he turned back and shut the patio door. "Not much of a view this morning," he said in a casual voice.

"The fresh air feels good." Were they going to pretend it hadn't happened? "Um, thank you for making breakfast."

"Rosita left homemade pecan rolls in the fridge. They're still baking. And you made the coffee. It was the least I could do." He settled into his chair and, thankfully, turned his gaze toward the wall of fog, his mug clutched between his hands as if it were a shield. "You didn't come back to bed last night," he said in a quiet voice.

Trish swallowed. She didn't know why this was so hard. She'd been a practicing grown-up since she'd been—what, five? She'd stared down hard men and defended her siblings and done everything in her power to escape the life her mother had. She could do this. She could have a completely rational conversation with a man she really, really liked who'd seen her naked. No sweat.

"Jane's teething. I got up several times. I didn't want to wake you up. One of us should sleep," she added weakly. Then she mentally kicked herself. Stop sounding weak! She was not weak!

"Ah," he said, in that same quiet voice. "I thought...I thought it might have been something to do with me. With something I did. Or didn't do."

She blinked at him. "No, it's not that. It's just..."

Words would be great. If only she had some.

"If I did something that you didn't like," he went on, "you can tell me. I promise, my ego can handle it."

But I don't know if I can handle it, she thought.

He sipped his coffee, patiently waiting for a reply from her. But then Jane pushed her bottle away and stretched her plump little arms over her head and began to whine and Trish was thankful for the distraction.

"Here," Nate said as Trish started to maneuver Jane onto her shoulder. "I've got her."

He got up and lifted Jane into his arms and began to rhythmically pat her on the back. He didn't sit back down, though. He went and stood at the edge of the patio, a few feet farther away from Trish.

He was over there thinking he'd been a lousy lover when the truth was, he'd been amazing. Trish stared into the fog, trying to pretend she wasn't about to say this out loud. "Actually, it was amazing. I didn't think it'd be that good."

Out of the corner of her eye, she saw him pause before he continued patting and rocking Jane. "Oh? Well. Good to know." He was trying to sound casual, but she could tell he was smiling, just by the tone of his voice.

Last weekend, she'd sat on this porch and decided not to tell him why she was so good with kids and why she wouldn't sleep with him. He hadn't needed to know, she'd rationalized then.

But now? After what they'd shared? "You want to hear the whole story?"

"I want to understand you."

Heat flooded her body and that tingling sensation tightened across her lower back again. This man seriously needed some flaws and fast.

"My father—or the man I think of as my father—left when I was four. My brothers Johnny and Danny were two and one, so I suppose that he might not have been my real father. But he's who I remember." She did manage to look at him. "They both joined the army the moment they were eligible. Johnny's down at Fort Hood and Danny's done a tour of Afghanistan."

"Then what happened?"

Trish closed her eyes. She could still feel the weight of Jane's small body against hers. Just like all the other small bodies that had lain in her arms. "There was a gap of about three years. I think my mom was trying, I really do. I remember being home alone a lot with Johnny and Danny. I got pretty good at opening cans and heating them up so we'd all have something to eat. Then, when I was seven, Clint happened."

"I take it that was not a good thing."

"Nope. Mom got pregnant again and…" she sighed, pushing back on the memory. "Mom had Millie but then Mom was never home so I got used to taking care of the baby. The boys started sleeping on the floor and Millie and I took the bed. Then Mom had Jeremiah. And there just wasn't enough food. Not for five of us."

"How old were you?"

"I was nine. Then Mom got pregnant again. And Hailey was not a healthy baby. I wound up skipping most of my sixth-grade year to take care of her."

"Your mom wouldn't take care of a sick baby? My mom quit her job teaching elementary school when we couldn't get Joe into a stable routine at school. My grandmother thought it'd be better for all of us if we put him in an institution, but Mom wouldn't hear of it. He was her son. It was her job to take care of him. It was all of our jobs."

She studied him. He really did seem pissed off at her mother. "Well, she did have a job. That helped. For a while, anyway. But no, she couldn't take care of Hailey. She couldn't really take care of any of us. But I could." She looked at Jane, who was falling into a milk coma on her uncle's shoulder. "I graduated with honors when I was twenty because of Hailey and Keith, who was born when I was fourteen. Keith…"

"Was he okay?"

"There was something wrong with him, with his heart. He died. When he was fourteen months old. I couldn't save him. And I always thought, you know——if we'd been able to get to a doctor, maybe…"

That *maybe* had haunted her for years. Just because, every single time her mother got knocked up by yet another man, Trish wanted to scream and cry and ask her what the hell she thought she was doing—it didn't mean she didn't do everything in her power to save that baby when he'd gotten here. But she'd only been fifteen. She had very little power to do anything. Including saving her little brother.

"I'm so sorry," Nate said. He'd grown quiet. "That must have been so hard on you."

Trish sniffed. "And that doesn't count Lenny, Ricky or Patsy. I left home when Patsy was five. It was the hardest thing I've ever done because I knew…" her words trailed off as her throat closed off. "Because I knew she'd be on her own. That I wouldn't be there to make sure she went to school or did her homework or had a real dinner every night."

"And your mom?"

"Oh, she's fine. She got her tubes tied after Patsy because the doctors said she couldn't have any more kids. She's…it's like she's my older sister, you know? Not my mom. My flighty older sister that's always screwing up. But the guy she's with now, Tim, he's a good guy. Good job, not rough. Helps take care of the kids. I hope he sticks around."

"Why did she do it? Why did she have so many kids when she couldn't take care of them? Because it wasn't fair of her to assume that you'd do it. It wasn't fair to you."

"Life is not fair. It never has been and it never will be. If it was, your mom wouldn't have had to quit to take care of your brother and Jane's parents would be on their way to pick her up right now and…" She almost said, "Diana wouldn't have cheated on you." But she didn't.

Nate sat down in his chair, Jane cuddled against his chest. "You don't—didn't—sleep with people because of your mom?"

"Yeah. She'd fall head over heels in love with some guy, have a couple of his babies, and then it'd all fall apart. I guess she thought the kids would help her hold onto a man, but it never worked that way. The funny thing is, she can't have kids with Tim and he's the one that's stuck around the longest. Seven years and counting."

The silence settled over them. She wondered how long his folks had been together. If he'd had an older brother… maybe thirty years? Maybe more?

"I don't want to be like her," Trish admitted, letting her words drift into the fog. "I don't want to be so in love with a man, so in love with sex with a man, that it becomes my whole world. I don't want to forget who I am. I don't want to have to be someone else to keep a man. I can do *so* much good in this world, more than just changing diapers."

"And to do that, you didn't get involved?"

"No." She swallowed, feeling unsure of herself. "It was easier that way. No distractions. I got off the rez, I got to college, I started the charity. And I…I can't give that up." *Not even for you*, she thought.

He turned Jane around so that the little girl was sitting on his lap, facing out into the fog. Trish saw that Jane was only half-awake, her eyelids fluttering with heaviness.

"So why didn't you come back to bed last night?" he asked softly.

"Because."

He snorted and finally turned to look at her. "That's not much of an answer."

She took a deep breath, but she didn't break his gaze. "Because I'm just the temporary nanny. I can't stay here with you forever. I can't give up my goals, my whole life, to play house with you. I can't turn into my mother and—I can't fall in love with you, Nate. I just *can't*."

"Ah," he exhaled, his eyebrows jumping up. "And you think that by sharing my bed you…might?"

She thought back to the way their bodies had fit together, how he'd made her feel alive and vibrant and perfect. How she'd wanted him again and again, how she'd felt like she was standing on the edge of a very tall cliff and all he'd have to do to get her to jump was ask.

"I might," she admitted.

If I haven't already.

Eleven

"So," Nate said in a voice that sounded remarkably calm, all things considered. "How would you like to proceed?"

"What do you mean?" Trish had turned her beautiful eyes back to the fog.

"With your remaining time here, assuming you'd like to finish out the three weeks."

She dropped her chin. "I don't want to break our deal," she said in a quiet voice. "I gave you my word just as much as you gave me yours."

Yeah, and part of his word had been *not* sleeping with her. That had lasted all of a week. Barely eight whole days.

He tried to think rationally, but that wasn't working. Because, rationally, not only should he have been able to stay away from her, but he should have been able to *keep* staying away from her.

He had to smile. How many other women in the world would take him to their beds and then tell him they couldn't come back because they couldn't risk falling for him and his billions in the bank? How many would keep their word to him?

Not that many. Maybe not any, except for Trish.

He ran his code as his tired brain tried to come up with a solution that didn't involve her leaving before the rolls were done in the oven.

"I can't leave," she said. "It'd be bad for Jane to go

through so many caretakers so fast. She's teething and
we're just getting into a rhythm and you don't have anyone else lined up."

Can't wasn't the same as *won't*. *Can't* made it sound like
he was forcing her and that was the last thing he wanted.
"This is all true, but I don't want that to be the only reason you stay."

"You're paying me," she reminded him.

That was better, he thought. She sounded a little more
like herself—more confident, more willing to push back.
Trish sounding vulnerable only made him want to fold her
into his arms and tell her he'd take care of everything, just
so long as she stayed with him.

"Insane amounts of money," she added. "Both in salary and in donations. That was the deal. I won't take your
money and run."

"The deal was we didn't sleep together. And now we
have. The deal is open for renegotiation."

A wary look crossed her face. "How do you mean?"

"Look, I'm going to be honest. I like you. A lot. And I
really enjoyed last night. You were amazing and it's going
to be hard to look at you every day and not want to take
you to bed every night."

She didn't immediately respond, which made him pretty
sure those weren't the right words. The fact that he was
making even a little bit of sense was a minor miracle, when
all he really wanted to do was deposit this sleepy baby back
in her crib and curl his body around Trish's and sleep for
another five or six hours.

He probably should tell her that hey, one-night stands
were fine and she knew where he was if she wanted another fun night in the sack—he should keep himself walled
off, above the situation, just like he always did when he
was out of his league.

But instead, no—he was laying it all on the line because, damn it, he liked her, he trusted her and, by God, she was someone he could fall for, too. For the first time in five years, waking up alone had bothered him. He'd wanted to see her face when he opened his eyes, to kiss her mouth awake.

He didn't want a casual one-night stand or even a casual one-week stand. It wasn't like he wanted to marry her or anything. He wasn't that old-fashioned. But he wanted something…in between.

He wanted a relationship.

From behind them, a buzzer sounded. "That's the rolls." He stood up, jostling Jane back from her semistupor as he handed the baby to Trish. "I'll be right back."

The rolls were slightly underdone, but that was good enough. He didn't want to stand in this kitchen for five more minutes while she was out there, talking herself out of another night of passionate sex with him. So he plated up the food and loaded everything onto the tray and tried his damnedest not to run right back to her.

If it came down to it, could he not touch her for another three weeks? He'd made it five years without taking a lover. Surely he could keep his hands—and other parts—occupied for another measly twenty-one days?

Jane had perked up a bit and Trish was singing and using the baby's chubby little legs to act out the song. It was a perfect image of what a family—his family—could be. Was it wrong to want more mornings like this? Breakfast on the patio, just the three of them?

He set the tray down and ate his breakfast while he waited. He'd respect her decision. He had no choice, because she was right. It would be hard on the baby if she left. It'd be hard on him, too, but he was a grown-ass man. He'd deal. Jane just needed more stability at this point in her life.

So this was parenthood, he realized as he burned the

roof of his mouth on a roll. Putting the baby's needs ahead of his own.

Stupid maturity.

Finally, after what seemed like ninety-nine verses, the song ended. Nate watched the two of them together. Jane clearly adored Trish—he hoped that, wherever she was, Elena would approve of his choice for a nanny.

And Trish was smiling down into Jane's face as if she really did care for the girl. Was it wrong to be attracted to a woman who would care so much for a child that had no connection to her?

Trish lifted her head and caught him staring. Her warm smile faded beneath a look of pensiveness. "How are the rolls?"

"Hot."

She managed a smirk so small, he almost missed it. "Shocking, that."

He forced himself to grin. "Come to any decisions over there?"

Jane squealed and tried to grab a roll. "I think," Trish said, capturing Jane's little fingers before they could get burned, "that we should finish this conversation during naptime."

That was a perfectly reasonable thing to say—after all, there was something a little weird about discussing sex with a baby around—but it still left him disappointed.

Jane trilled again.

"Right. Naptime. Looking forward to it."

Trish hesitated in the doorway of the parlor long enough that Nate looked up from the book he was reading. "She go to sleep okay?"

"Yes."

Nate was sitting on one end of the couch, close to the

leather chair. She could either sit in the leather chair or next to him.

He closed his book and waited for her to make her choice.

So she stood. "I feel like I owe you an apology," she said. "I've never had an affair before. I don't feel like I'm handling myself very well."

"An affair. Is that what this is?"

"Isn't it?"

"Right now it's closer to a one-night stand. Without the standing," he added as her cheeks heated. "An affair implies more than one night together."

"Oh, okay." Right. She couldn't even get her terminology right. Yeah, she was pretty bad at this. "About that." She forced herself to take another step into the room.

"Yes?" He sat up and, putting the book aside, leaned forward. But he didn't come toward her, he didn't sweep her into his arms and say the kinds of things that might weaken her resolve. He just waited for her to choose.

"I'd like—I mean, I think I'd like to, you know, maybe have an affair." Calling it an affair made it sound sophisticated and glamorous—nothing like the wild, indiscriminate coupling her mother engaged in. Trish was a responsible woman who could have an affair with a handsome, wealthy, powerful man *without* losing her head—or her heart.

She hoped.

The corner of his mouth crooked up. "You don't sound certain."

"I just want to make sure things don't get complicated. Messy," she explained.

"You don't want to fall," he clarified for her. The way he said it made her feel like she'd rejected him, which didn't make a lot of sense.

Wasn't she agreeing to the affair? How was that re-

jecting him? He didn't expect her to fawn over him, did
he? "I don't want to fall," she said firmly. She could do
this—indulge in a little passion without losing herself.
She would *not* fall.

Falling in love with Nate Longmire was not a part of
the plan.

"I've been thinking about that."

"You have?"

He nodded and stood. "Just you and me and a casual
affair."

Casual. That was both the right word and not at all.
"How would we do that?"

"We could have some…rules. Guidelines, if you will.
No spending the night, no funny business when Jane is
awake—"

"Right. Guidelines." She liked the sound of that. Bound-
aries. Like the three weeks they had left. That was a bound-
ary that would keep her from falling in a very real way.
Nate would hire another nanny and Trish would move out
and that space—*that* would keep her from falling. It had
to. "Nothing in front of Rosita or Stanley or anyone. And
no seeing other people while we're being casual, right?"

"Sure." He grinned at her. "I doubt either of us would
have, anyway."

"I suppose not." She felt herself exhale a little. She
knew she wasn't doing a bang-up job at this, but it didn't
appear she was botching it beyond all hope. "What else?"

"Just this." Suddenly, Nate was moving, his long legs
closing the distance between them and his hands cupping
her cheeks. He was kissing her so hard that her knees didn't
entirely hold her up. "Just that I'm glad you said yes," he
whispered against her mouth.

"Oh, Nate," she breathed as his lips trailed down her
neck. This desire she felt—this need—surely this wasn't
a bad thing, right? This wasn't the kind of thing that was

going to push everything she'd ever worked for aside. Right?

They had guidelines to help keep everything from spiraling out of control. She could have an affair with Nate, enjoy being with him and sleeping with him.

And she would do it without falling.

They settled into a routine after that. Trish couldn't bring herself to sleep with Nate when Jane was down for a nap, but that didn't stop her from kissing him. She'd never even made out before, so just tangling up with Nate on the couch or against the counter in the kitchen, or when they caught each other on the stairs—anywhere, really, where Rosita wouldn't walk in on them—was a gift. A gift that left her in a near-constant state of arousal.

So by the time she closed Jane's door for the night, Trish could hardly wait to get her hands on him.

And he was ready for her. Instead of the leisurely kissing and touching that happened during the day, they would rip off each other's clothes and fall into bed as fast as they could.

Nate did not disappoint. The more they made love, the better it got. After the first week, when he'd introduced her to most of the basics, he started asking her what she wanted—what she'd always wanted to try, what she was curious about. For so long, Trish hadn't even acknowledged that she *had* sexual desires—if she didn't cop to them, then she didn't really have them. So suddenly to have a man who not only was interested in her, but also interested in making sure her fantasies were fulfilled was sometimes more than she could handle. It took her three days to admit that she wanted to go down on him—in the shower. Which he was more than happy to help her try out.

Nate didn't push her, though. And he didn't complain

when, after they were panting and sated, she gathered up her clothes and went back to her own bedroom.

Which got harder every night. The more time they spent in each other's arms, the more she wanted to wake up in his arms.

And the more she wanted to do that, the more she *had* to go back to her side of the hallway. Because she knew what was happening.

Despite the guidelines, despite the routine—despite it all—she was falling for him. And that scared the hell out of her.

Because there was only a week to go until her time was up.

She had no idea how she was going to leave.

Twelve

Trish turned to him as the door shut behind the third and final nanny candidate, a squat Polish grandmother with impeccable references. The first candidate was a middle-aged former receptionist who'd been laid off in the Great Recession and the second was a young woman about Trish's age who just "loved kids!"—as she so enthusiastically phrased it.

"Well?" Trish said, leaning against the closed door with her hands behind her back. "What did you think?"

"I think I should hire you to do all my interviews," Nate said, moving in on her and pinning her to the door with a kiss. She'd grilled each woman on schedules, sleeping philosophies and life-saving qualifications. All Nate had had to do was watch. "You're ruthless."

"I just want the best for Jane." She pushed him back, but she was smiling as she did it. "Rosita will see us," she scolded quietly.

"I don't care." And he didn't. It was Friday. He only had Trish here for another three days. Monday morning, the new nanny would start. Trish would move out. She'd come back to help settle the new nanny into the routine on Wednesday, if needed, but that was it.

He kissed her again, feeling her body respond to his. Three more days of feeling her tongue tracing his lips, her body molding itself to his. And then...

She pushed him back again. "Nate," she said in her most disapproving voice, even as her fingers fluttered over his shoulders. "Focus. You need to pick a new nanny from the three candidates."

"Do I have to?"

She gave him a look. He knew he sounded childish, but picking a new nanny put him that much closer to not having Trish around anymore. If there were any way to stall hiring her replacement, she'd have to stay, right?

Because he wanted her to stay.

He and Trish had not spent a great deal of time talking about what happened next. He wanted to keep seeing her, obviously. The past month had been something he hadn't even allowed himself to dream of. The sex was amazing, sure, but what he felt for her went beyond the physical. He connected with her in a way that he hadn't connected with another woman—another person—since he'd fallen for Diana almost ten years ago. This time, he was older, smarter—more ready for it. This wasn't a casual affair, not anymore. This was a relationship—the one he wanted.

Yes, they'd had these guidelines that were supposed to keep her from falling for him. Unfortunately, nothing had prevented *him* from falling for *her*.

Because he'd fallen, hard. Unlike when he'd met Diana, Nate knew he wasn't with Trish just because she was the best he thought he could do. He wasn't the same insecure geek he'd been back in college. He could have his pick of women, if he really wanted to. They'd line up for him, starting with Lola Finklestein.

That wasn't what he wanted. He just wanted Trish. He missed her like hell when she was in class every Tuesday and Thursday and it no longer had to do with his panic over Jane. He could take care of Jane now. He'd learned her different noises and her likes and dislikes and he was doing a passable job at changing diapers—all because

Trish had patiently walked him through the ins and outs of basic fatherhood.

He wanted to be a better man for her. Every night he tried to show her how much he cared for her, how much he wanted her to stay with him. And every night, she slipped away from him again.

When he tried to bring up the prospect of dating, she kept shutting down on him. He knew that she had made arrangements to crash with a friend for the remaining week and a half until she graduated, and then she planned to go home and see her family for a while. But beyond that...

"You pick," he told her as he traced his fingertips down her cheek. "I trust your opinion."

"Nate. You *have* to pick. I'm—"

"Señor Nate?" Rosita called from the kitchen. "I am going to do the shopping." Nate stepped clear of Trish just as Rosita walked out of the kitchen, her purse on her arm. "Is there anything that..." Her eyes darted between Trish and Nate. "Ah, anything you want?" she finished in a suspicious voice.

"No. You?" he asked Trish.

"Maybe another box of those teething biscuits Jane likes?" Trish suggested. She managed to sound perfectly normal, but she couldn't stop the blush.

"*Sí,*" Rosita said, a look Nate couldn't quite make out on her face.

Trish stepped away from the door so Rosita could pass. Nate caught the small smile Rosita threw to Trish, and then the housekeeper was out the door. "What was that about?"

"I think we've been busted." Trish frowned at the closed door.

"Does that mean we don't have to sneak around anymore?" As he said it, he moved back to her, wrapping his arms around her waist and resting his chin on the top of her head. They stood like that for a while, just enjoying each other's warmth. They had time. Jane was still down for her nap. And later, they'd load her into the stroller and go for a walk. Then, tonight, she'd come to his bed again.

It was a damn good life. One he didn't want to end. Not in three days, not in three months. Maybe not in forever.

He had to find a way to make her stay. The sooner, the better.

"Nate." She looked up at him and rested the tips of her fingers just above the line of his stubble. "You have to decide. Not me, not Stanley and not Rosita. *You*. It's your choice."

Suddenly, he didn't know if they were talking about the three nanny candidates or if she was talking about them.

"I already found the perfect woman," he told her, tightening his arms around her. "You." He took a deep breath. This was the moment. He wasn't going to let her slip away from him. He *needed* her. "You should stay."

She tensed in his arms. "That's not what I mean."

"Why not?" She started to slip out of his grasp, but this time, he didn't let her go. He put his hands on her shoulders and turned her to face him. "Trish. Look at me."

Almost as if she was doing so against her will, she raised her gaze to meet his. He was surprised to see that she looked…afraid?

He was all in. "I want you to stay."

"I can't," she said in such a quiet whisper that he barely heard her. "Oh, Nate—don't ask me this. I can't."

"Why not?" he demanded. "Jane loves you," She sucked in a hard breath and her eyes began to shine with wetness. "I'm falling in love with you," he went on. "You fit here."

"No, I don't. Can't you see?" She laughed, a sharp thing that cut him. "I grew up in a three-room house with mold growing up the walls and electricity that only worked some of the time. I slept in a bed with two or three little kids my entire life. We didn't have food. We didn't have things."

She waved her hands around her, at all the nice things he had. "And now? I'm still so poor that I buy all my clothes from a thrift store and before I moved in here, I lived on ramen noodles and generic cereal—that I ate dry because I couldn't afford milk. I do *not* fit here." Her voice dropped. "I don't fit *you*, Nate. Not really. This was…an affair. A casual affair between two people living in forced proximity. That's—" Her voice caught. "That's all this was."

"No, it wasn't. You fit me," he said, beginning to feel desperate. "You fit *me*, Trish. We can change everything else. Anything you want. Name it. I won't let you go back to living on the edge like that. Not when I can take care of you. Not when I need you." He cupped her face in his hands. "I need you, Trish."

"You need—" She gulped. "You need a nanny."

"Stop it, Trish. You know that's not true. I need *you*. You're not some interchangeable woman. I can't just swap you out and carry on as if nothing has changed. I'm different when I'm with you. I'm not nervous or geeky or nothing but a bank account. You make me *me*. You make me feel like everything's finally right in the world."

She closed her eyes and shook her head. "Oh, Nate. Don't make this harder than it has to be. We had a deal, you and I. A temporary nanny. A casual affair. That was the plan. No falling."

The desperation turned and suddenly he was mad. Why was she being so stubborn? She had feelings for him, he knew she did. He gripped her by the arms. "I want a new deal. I want a different plan."

"Don't do this," she whispered again, trying to back away from him, but he held tight. "*Don't*. I can't fall."

"What's it going to take, Trish? To get you to stay. Twenty thousand a month? Two hundred and fifty thousand for your charity? That was our deal, right? I want an extension on our contract."

"Nate."

She was trying to cut him off, trying to stop him, but what did billions in the bank mean if he couldn't take care of her? If he couldn't make sure that she never felt poor ever again?

If he couldn't get her to stay?

She was worth more than that to him. She was worth more than all of it. All that cash was pointless if it couldn't get him what he really wanted—her. "Anything you want, name it. Just…stay with me, Trish."

Too late, he realized he'd gone too far.

"Oh, Nate." She shook free of his grasp and looked up at him. Tears streamed out of the corners of her eyes. "I—I can't. I can't give up everything I've ever been, everything I've ever wanted to accomplish, to raise another baby that's not mine. There's so much more I need to do in this world right now and I can't sacrifice all of that, not yet." Her eyes filled with tears. "I'm not ready to be a mother. Not even a mother. A nanny."

"You're more than that to me, babe. You know that."

She shook her head. Why couldn't he make her see reason? "I can't turn my back on my own family, my tribe, just to play house with you."

"This isn't playing house. I want you to live with me. I want you to sleep in my bed with me." Why was that a bad thing? He didn't understand. "I want more than casual. I want more than an affair. I want *you.*"

"On your terms, Nate. We aren't equals. We can *never* be equals." Her voice broke.

Where had he gone wrong? Since when had telling a woman he loved her become such a mess? Panic bubbled just beneath his surface, threatening to break free. He'd never been that good with women, never known what to say to them. That'd been what he loved about Trish—he could talk to her. But not right now. His words were failing him.

"I would always be dependent on you," she went on, her face pale. "I would always need you more than you needed me."

"That's not true."

She smiled at him, a weak and sad smile that hurt to see. "Just because you can't see that doesn't mean it's not true." She touched his face but pulled her hand away quickly, as if she'd been burned. "I…I can't need you as much as this."

"Why not?" He said louder than he meant to, but was she being serious? "I need you, too. That doesn't make me weak and it doesn't make you weak, for God's sake. It makes me want to take care of *you*. So let me."

She stood before him, her face creased with pain. Then, unexpectedly, she leaned up on her toes and kissed him. For a moment, he thought that was her giving in, her agreeing to stay. He tried to wrap his arms around her to hold her tight. *Thank God*, he thought.

Then she was away from him. "Of *course* I care for you," she said, skirting around him. "I could love you for the rest of my days."

"Could?" he asked incredulously as she started up the stairs.

"But I can't lose myself in you. I can't…." A sob broke free of her chest and she stopped, four steps up. "I can't forget who I am."

"I'm not asking you to do that. Damn it, Trish—I'm asking you to stay!"

She turned, looking down on him with a face full of pain. He started up the stairs to reach for her, but she backed away from him. "If I agree to your new terms—if I agree to stay—then what? Another month passes, we fall more in love, you extend the contract again, one month at a time."

"Don't you want to stay with us?" he demanded. "Isn't that what you want?"

"Oh, God, of course I do. But this isn't real, don't you see? All of this," she said as she swept her arms around, "and…you—God, Nate." Her voice caught in another sob. "People are depending on me. I have things I *have* to do."

"So do them from here!"

She shook her head. "I can't. I can't be your kept woman. I—I have to go."

Before he could do anything else, she spun and raced up the stairs, her shoulders shaking under the strain of her sobs.

What the hell? Okay, so he shouldn't have brought money into the conversation. That was a mistake, one he wouldn't make again. But…

A kept woman? That wasn't what was happening here! He was in love with her, for God's sake! And she might be in love with him, too—wasn't that what she'd said when she'd said she could love him the rest of her life?

So what was the problem here?

Overhead, he heard her door shut—and the lock click. He could go after her, go in through Jane's room. He could make her see reason—

And what? Argue with her until she agreed just to keep the peace? Force her to stay?

He sat heavily on the steps, pulled down by a weight in the center of his chest. For some reason, his brain decided that this would be the perfect time to revisit Diana's betrayal. To remember walking into the house that was supposed to be empty and hearing the distinctive noises of sex. To remember reasoning that it was just Brad with his latest girl. To remember calling Diana's phone to see where she was—and hearing it ring from the coat stand right at his elbow.

To remember walking up the stairs in his parents' home,

each footstep heavier than the last. Opening the door to his brother's room and seeing Diana, naked and bouncing on top of Brad.

Realizing with crushing certainty that he'd screwed up somewhere along the line—that he hadn't been enough for her. He'd been good enough until someone better came along.

He'd closed himself off after that. He didn't let himself get close to people, to women, because he couldn't be sure they weren't after something else—his company, his money.

He'd let himself get close to Trish. He'd trusted her with a part of himself he'd held back from every other person. He'd let himself be more real with her than he'd been in… years. Maybe in forever. He'd let himself think that he was enough for her. Him, Nate Longmire. Not the Boy Billionaire, not the philanthropist who cut the checks. Just him.

And what had she done?

She'd decided he wasn't enough. He wasn't enough; Jane wasn't enough. The two of them could never be more important to Trish than a bunch of backpacks.

He wasn't more important than two new pencils. Not to her.

Damn, but that hurt.

Trish packed quickly. Anything to not think about what had just happened. What was still happening.

Nate…

The moment she felt herself waver, she pushed back. Her mother would do anything to keep a man happy. Her mother would quit her job, ignore her children—anything, as long as it kept her man coming back for more.

And Trish? She could do it. She could agree to what Nate wanted, when he wanted it, as long as he kept on loving her. Even that last kiss—it'd almost broken her resolve.

She couldn't do it. She couldn't give herself over to him and cast everything that she'd held dear to the wind.

So she packed as fast as she could. She couldn't stay, not a moment longer. Every second she was around Nate was another second of temptation. Another second she would break.

It didn't take that long. Since she'd completed her schoolwork, she'd sold most of her books back already. She only had a few that were worth keeping more than they were worth the few dollars she'd get at the bookstore.

Her clothes fit into the duffel. She packed up her laptop, her shoes and the phone.

No, the phone was his. She didn't need it, didn't need the constant reminder of how Nate wanted to take care of her. If she kept his phone... Besides, they didn't get a lot of cell-phone reception on the rez, anyway. Who would she call, except him? She put it back on the dock.

What was she doing? This whole thing was ridiculous. It'd been ridiculous since she'd first agreed to his contract. She had no business being in this nice house, surrounded by nice people and things and food. But more than the material comforts, she had no business being in Nate's bed, having a casual affair. She had absolutely no business being with a man who was going to break her heart.

She couldn't stay. She couldn't give herself over to him, mind, body and soul. She could not lose who she was to become the woman he loved. That was what her mother did.

That's not what Trish did. She shared a name and a physical resemblance with her mother, but that's where it ended. Trish was a strong woman with a plan.

A plan that had never included falling in love with Nate. Except she had. She *had*.

She buried her head in her hands, trying not to sob. She'd been wondering if maybe it wouldn't be such a bad thing to stay for another two weeks—finish out the school year living here, taking the comfort of Nate's bed—until she went home for a couple of months. She'd been sorely tempted. It was just another twelve, fourteen days at the most. Where was the harm in that? And then, after she'd spent some time away from Nate, she'd be in a better position to figure out how she wanted to proceed with him. Because she hadn't been done. She'd just…needed to get some perspective to make sure she didn't lose herself in him.

How had this happened? That was the problem. Somewhere, the attraction she'd felt at their first meeting had blossomed into something else, something infinitely more. Watching Nate cuddle Jane? Eating breakfasts out on his patio? Talking about comic books and charities?

Lying in his arms at night? All those stolen moments during the day?

A month ago, she hadn't loved him. A month ago, the little girl still sleeping in the next room had been in dire straits, only days from a trip to the emergency room.

A month ago, everything had been different.

Including Trish.

She was not her mother's daughter. No matter how much she wanted to open that door and run down to him and tell him that she was sorry and he was right and she'd do anything he wanted, just so long as he said he loved her and he kept on loving her. She wouldn't.

She had to walk away. Before she lost herself completely.

Her things packed up into two sad bags, Trish forced herself to go through the bathroom to Jane's room. The little girl was restless, although her eyes were still closed. She'd probably picked up on the sudden tension in the house, Trish thought.

"You're a good girl," she told the drowsy baby as she stroked the fine hairs on her little head for the last time.

"You take good care of your uncle Nate, okay? Make sure to smile at him and make him laugh like you do, okay?"

Jane shook her head from side to side, as if she was trying to tell Trish to stay, too.

"He's going to be a great daddy for you," Trish went on. "He loves you and he'll take good care of you." She thought back to all the times Nate had cuddled Jane or changed her or fed her—all the times he'd been a father.

All the times she'd been so surprised that he would be a father to someone else's child only because she didn't know men would do such things.

She leaned down and kissed Jane's head. "Goodbye, Jane. I love you. I won't forget you." The thought made her start to cry again because she knew that Jane would never remember her.

She hurried back to her room—no, it wasn't hers. It was merely the room she'd slept in for a month. Nothing here was hers, except for the sad duffels. She hefted them onto her shoulders and, with one last look, headed out.

As she trudged down the stairs, part of her brain was screaming at her that she was being stubborn—she didn't have to go! So Nate had been less than smooth. He wasn't always, she knew that. She was overreacting and she should let him take care of her.

But she was so much more than a temporary nanny with benefits. She ran a charity that hundreds, maybe thousands of children depended on for food and school supplies and the chance at a life better than the ones they'd been born into. She owed it to those kids—the ones who would never have a billionaire uncle to suddenly show up and make everything better—to do her best for them. For Patsy, her littlest sister. Trish was defined by her actions, not by the man she was sleeping with. She'd told him she would not fall for him and, at least on the surface, she had to hold that line.

She was a temporary nanny who'd had a casual affair and now it was time to go back to her real life. That's all there was to it.

Nate was waiting for her at the bottom of the stairs, hands on his hips. Just the sight of him nearly broke her resolve. *Be strong*, she told herself. Her mother would cave. She was not her mother.

But this was Nate. Her Nate. The man who'd said he was falling for her...

"I want you to stay, Trish," he said in a voice that was almost mean.

In that moment, she buckled. He was everything she wanted but... *Be strong*, she told herself. "You'll be all right? You and Jane? For the weekend?"

He stared at her as if she were speaking Lakota instead of English. "Don't we mean *anything* to you? How can you just walk away from her? From *me*?"

"I...I have to do this." Her own excuses rang hollow because he was right. Jane meant something to her. She wasn't just a baby that Trish had to take care of because no one else would.

And Nate? He wasn't just a man—any man, like her mother would have settled for. He was a man who stepped up when he had to. He took an active role in his niece's care. He didn't just take from Trish—he listened to her, he made her feel important.

"And that's it?" He made a sweeping gesture with his hands, as if he could clear everything away. "That's *that*?"

He was breaking her heart. For so long, she'd guarded herself against just this—the pain that went with the end. That's what her mother had taught her. It always ended and when it did, it always hurt. Every single time.

"I don't know," she admitted. "We just—I need some space. This has been a *great* month," she hurried to add, "but everything's happened so fast and I need to step back and make sure that I'm not losing myself. I've got to graduate and go home for a while. Maybe for the summer, I don't know. And after that…"

"Will you call me? At least let me know where you wind up tonight, so I won't worry about you."

Oh, God. Somehow, admitting this was almost as hard as leaving because it felt so *final*. No calls, no texts. A definitive break. "I left the phone upstairs."

All the blood drained out of his face. He knew it, too. "Oh. Okay. I see."

"Nate…"

"I, uh, I called for a car. It'll take you wherever you want to go."

"Thank you." She didn't know what else to say. She'd never broken up with anyone before. She'd only seen the screaming, crying fights her mother had had. He was being polite and respectful and, well, Nate.

Then, unexpectedly, he stepped up the few stairs separating them and cupped her face in his palms and touched his forehead to hers. She was powerless to stop him. "You probably don't want me to say this, but I don't care. I love you, Trish. Think about that when you go home. *I love you*. It doesn't make me less to love you. It makes me want to be someone *more* than who I was before I met you."

She gasped and closed her eyes against the tears. She couldn't do this, couldn't break his heart and hers—

Outside, a car horn honked.

Nate moved again, but instead of kissing her, he grabbed one of her bags and carried it down the rest of the way. He opened the door for her.

Struggling to breathe, Trish picked up the other bag and walked out into the weak afternoon sunshine.

It'd always been easy to stick to her principles, to keep herself safe from the messy entanglements that had ruled her childhood and all the children that they'd produced.

But putting her few belongings in the back of the trunk of some hired car? Silently standing there as Nate opened the backseat door for her? *Not* telling him she'd changed her mind when he leaned down and said, "I'll wait for you," right before he closed the door?

"Where to?" the driver said.

No, nothing about this was easy.

But she did it, anyway. She would not live month to month, at the mercy of this deal or that. She would *not* be ruled by love.

"San Francisco State University," she told the driver in a raw voice.

And that was that.

Thirteen

The day of graduation dawned bright and hot. Trish was already sweating in her cap and gown. Underneath she had on a pair of cutoffs and her Wonder Woman shirt. It was foolish to hope that the shirt would imbue her with enough power to make it through all the speeches and waiting to finally cross that damn stage and get her master's degree without dying of heatstroke, but it was the best she had.

"Who's the speaker, again?" Trish asked her neighbor after she took her seat in Cox Stadium.

"I don't know," the woman replied. "It was supposed to be Nancy Pelosi, but they said she canceled at the last minute."

"Great." Trish pulled out the water bottle she'd hidden in the sleeves of her master's gown and took a long drink.

As the university president and student body president made remarks about everyone's dedication in achieving their chosen master's degrees—the undergraduates were graduating tomorrow—and how their true potential could now be unlocked and so on and so on and *so on*, Trish only paid the bare minimum of attention. She was running through her plans.

Somehow, Stanley had tracked her down in the library. He'd brought her three checks—one for twenty grand and another for two hundred and fifty thousand, made out to

One Child, One World. The last one had been her security deposit from Mrs. Chan. All he'd said when he found her was, "You doing okay?"

"Yes, I'm fine. Nate, is he okay?" she'd asked in a rush. "Is Jane okay?"

"She's fine." Stanley had given her a look that she couldn't interpret before saying, "And Nate, well, he's been better." Stanley handed her a padded envelope. Then the tattooed, pierced man was off again, leaving Trish alone with a vague sense of guilt as she looked at the hundreds of thousands of dollars in her hands.

She'd opened the padded envelope to find her phone and the charger. The phone was charged and she had a waiting text message.

Just in case. Nate.

She'd sat staring at the phone for a good twenty minutes. Just in case.

Just in case she wanted to call him. Just in case she changed her mind.

That was almost as unbelievable as the rest of it. All those men her mother had "loved"? All of them had had someone on the side. None of them had ever kept their promises, except for Tim.

Except for Nate.

Then she'd all but sprinted to her bank. Because she was now rich, comparatively, she was going to buy an actual plane ticket to Rapid City, South Dakota, instead of taking the bus. From there, she'd figure out a way to get home. It might take her a few days, but she'd make it there one way or another.

And after she'd been home for a few days...well, she

had to see how it went. She didn't plan on staying on the rez, but she had no apartment in San Francisco to come back to. After today, she had nothing to tie her to this city except Nate. If her father still lived here, she hadn't found him and he hadn't found her. She could make a fresh start somewhere new—somewhere with cheaper rents—or...or she could come back to Nate. If he'd still have her.

"I'll wait for you," he'd said when he'd closed her car door. She desperately wanted to believe him but at the same time, she was afraid to get her hopes up, afraid to think that there really was a future between them.

Because how would it work? She didn't even have a proper job lined up. If—and that was a big *if*—she went back to him, she wanted to walk up to that door on her own merits, not because she was crawling back.

But she had no idea how to level the playing field—the huge, gaping playing field—that existed between them.

She was getting ahead of herself. Before she could even think about that, she had to get through the next few days. The idea of getting on a plane was a terrifying one—so terrifying that, when the commencement speaker was announced, she didn't hear the name. But someone behind her whooped and then the crowd was cheering. Trish looked up to see...

Nate.

Nate Longmire, wearing a fancy cap and gown, strode out onto the stage and shook the university president's hands.

Oh, God, was all she could think before he stepped up to the microphone. What was he doing here? This couldn't be a coincidence—could it? No. This was intentional. This was because of her.

"Congratulations, graduates!" he said with one of those

tight smiles that she recognized as him being nervous. "I know you're all disappointed that Congresswoman Pelosi was unable to make it—" There were a variety of muffled groans from the audience. "But," Nate went on, ignoring the noise, "I had such a great time here about two months ago that I jumped at the chance to talk to you one more time."

Sporadic applause erupted. Someone wolf-whistled.

"Today I want to talk about the power each and every one of you possess," Nate continued. Even she could see him blushing at this distance. "You may be sitting there, asking yourselves, 'now what?' You may have student debt. You may not have a job. Maybe you've got someone, maybe you broke up."

"Oh, hell."

She didn't realize she'd spoken out loud until the woman sitting on her left said, "What?"

"Oh. Sorry. Nothing." Nothing except that her last— her only—lover was up on stage, slowly circling his way through a commencement speech that was all about her.

"You may not think you have any power to change things—to get a job in this economy, to find the 'right' person, to affect change in your surroundings. I'm here to tell you that's not true."

"You okay?" the woman on her left asked. "You don't look so good."

"I'm—fine. I'm fine." Trish forced herself to look away from Nate and smile at her neighbor. "I just can't believe Nate Longmire is up there, that's all."

The woman smiled. "He's even better-looking in person."

"Yes," Trish agreed weakly. "Better in person."

"I recently spent some time with a SFSU graduate by

the name of Trish Hunter," Nate was saying. As he talked, he searched the crowd until his gaze fell upon hers. The corner of his mouth moved and she knew he was glad to see her.

She wasn't sure if she was breathing or not—she was definitely light-headed. What was he *doing*?

"I was impressed with her education but more than that, I was impressed with her dedication. Despite a limited amount of funds, Ms. Hunter has single-handedly run a charity called One Child, One World, which provides school supplies and meals to Native American children living in poverty on reservations in South Dakota."

The audience settled back into their heat-induced stupor as he went on about her charity, her awards and, yes, her dedication. Trish couldn't do anything but gape at him. This wasn't happening, was it? Maybe she'd just had a heatstroke and was hallucinating this whole thing.

He was really here. He was—well, he was fighting for her. No one had ever fought for her before, not like this. She'd known he wasn't the same kind of man her mother had always chased—but this?

He wasn't going to run away. He wasn't going to hide behind lies.

Something Tim, her stepfather, had said to her the last time they'd talked floated back into her consciousness— "There's something about being with her that makes me feel right with the world. And when you've seen as much of the world as I have, you know that's no small thing."

The epiphany hit her so hard she jolted in her chair. Her mother—her flighty, careless mother who chased after any man she could catch—had been happily married for almost seven years to a decent guy who wouldn't even let Trish give him back a security deposit. She'd stayed married to him because they made each other feel right with the world.

Nate had said it himself. "You make me feel like everything's finally right in the world," he'd told her during the last few moments she'd stood before him and wavered.

And Tim was right—it was no small thing. It was something huge. It might be everything.

Would she really keep pushing herself away from Nate just because her mother had a long, scarred history of making bad choices? Or was Trish forcing herself to make a bad choice, just because it was the opposite of what her mother would have done?

Did Nate make everything right in her world, too?

"And so," Nate finally said, "I am happy to announce that the Longmire Foundation will be awarding two endowments. The first is to establish a scholarship for Native American students who enroll in San Francisco State University. The other is an endowment of ten million dollars to One Child, One World to help prepare those Native students for college and beyond."

Trish shot to her feet and tried to ask him what the *hell* he was doing, but all that came out of her mouth was a gurgling noise.

"Ah, yes, there she is, ladies and gentlemen. Please give Ms. Hunter a round of applause for all her hard work."

The crowd broke out into what could only be called a standing ovation as people cheered for her. She barely heard it. All she heard was Nate leaning forward and saying, "Ms. Hunter, if I could speak to you after you graduate?"

"That's you?" the woman on her left said. "Girl, you better move."

But Trish couldn't because she was trapped in the hell

of having a last name that started with an *H*. All she could
do was go through the motions. The rest of the graduation
passed in an absolute blur. Trish didn't remember hearing
her name called, barely remembered walking across the
stage to get her diploma. She did, however, have full recall of when some university higher-up pulled her out of
the line that was moving back toward the seats and ush-
ered her off the stage. "…Very exciting," he was saying as
he led Trish to where Nate was waiting. "An endowment!
This is excellent news…"

Nate was waiting for her in the shadows under the
stands of the stadium, cap in hand and gown unzipped. He
had on a button-up shirt and a tie and he looked *so* good.

Suddenly, Trish was very conscious of the fact that she
was in cutoffs and a T-shirt. Just another way they didn't
match up.

"What did you do?" she demanded the moment Nate
was in earshot.

He grinned at her as if he'd expected her to say that, but
then he turned to the official. "If I could have a moment
with Ms. Hunter…"

"Oh, yes. Yes, of course!" The man hurried back into
the sunlight, still muttering, "Excellent news!" as he de-
parted.

And then she and Nate were alone. "What did you *do*,
Nate?"

"I removed the money from the equation."

"By giving me ten freaking million dollars? Are you
insane? That's not removing it—that's putting it front and
center!"

"No, I didn't. I gave your charity the money, free and
clear. No strings attached. You'll be able to draw a salary as the head of the charity and do all those things you

wanted to do—basketball courts and after-school snacks and computer labs. All of it."

He hadn't forgotten her wish list. Why did that make her feel so good? "What do you mean, no strings? You just *gave* me ten million dollars!" Her voice echoed off the bottoms of the stands.

"No, I didn't," he repeated with more force. "I divested myself of some of my money to a worthy charity. I do that all the time."

"But—but—"

He touched her then, pulling her deeper into the shadows. "I gave *you* a choice."

"What?"

"I want you to come back to me," he said, dropping his voice down. "But I don't ever want you to feel that you're not my equal, that you're not good enough for me. And I sure as hell don't ever want you to feel that I hold all the cards. So, here we are. I give your charity money that I'll never miss and you'll do so much good with it—and you'll be able to pay yourself a salary." He grinned. "Knowing you, it won't be very much, but still."

"I don't see what this has to do with you giving me a *choice*, Nate. How is this not the same deal as before?"

In the safety of the shadows, he trailed his fingers down the side of her face. "This money is for your charity. It's not contingent on you moving back in with me. That's what no-strings-attached means. I won't take this money back—in fact, I believe certain government regulations would frown upon it. No matter what happens next, the charity gets the money. *That's* the deal."

"But—"

"If you want to come back to me—or if you want me to come to wherever you are—then you and I will both know that it's not because you couldn't say no to the money. You won't have to rely on me. You will be your own woman. That's what you want, isn't it?"

"I want…" She had to lean away from his touch. "But it won't change the fact that the money came from you."

"I doubt that any of those kids on the rez will give a damn where the money came from," he said in a matter-of-fact voice. "And you're missing the *if*. *If* you come back to me. It's your choice. It always has been."

"Nate…"

"I messed up the negotiations last time," he went on. "A good negotiator always knows what the other side wants and the first time, you wanted funding. It was easy to give it to you because all I needed was a nanny. But the second time, that's not what you wanted and I should have known it because I didn't want you as a nanny anymore. The situation had changed."

"You…didn't?"

"You wanted something else—you told me yourself. You didn't want to lose yourself in me. I didn't figure out what that meant at first." He grinned and despite the fact that she'd been yelling at him, he still looked thrilled to see her. "But I think I've got it now."

"What?" Her words failed her. She knew she was repeating herself, but she couldn't get a grasp on this situation.

"I think you wanted a promise," he said, going down on one knee in the shadows under the stadium bleachers. "A promise that I would honor your wishes—that I would honor *you*—with no strings attached. I didn't give that to you then. But I'd like to try again." He reached into his pocket and pulled out a small, bright blue box. The size that usually held a ring.

The air stopped moving in her lungs as he opened the box. "What are you doing, Nate?"

"Making you a promise," he said. A splendid pear-shaped diamond was nestled on a silver band. "Trish Hunter, will you marry me?"

Her mouth opened, but no sound came out as she looked from the ring—the promise—back to him.

"I want to marry you. I hope you want to marry me." He cracked a nervous little grin. "It usually works better that way."

"But I was going to go home!"

"I want you to go." He stood and, taking her hand in his, slipped the ring on her finger. "I want you to think about this, about us. I don't want you to come back to me because you're worried about Jane or you think you owe me. I don't want you to lose yourself. I want you as you've been. You push back when I do something dumb, you teach me how to do things. You make me a real person, Trish—not some caricature of a billionaire geek with too much money. You give me a purpose. You make everything feel right in my world and that's something I honestly wouldn't ever get back."

"You're not that—not to me," she told him, her words getting caught in the back of her throat. "You're just Nate and you're a wonderful man. I'm—I'm afraid, Nate. I'm *afraid*. I don't have any great role models for how to make a relationship work. I spent so long not being in one that to suddenly fall in love with you? You were my first. And when I was with you, I didn't feel like the same person I'd always defined myself as—the poor American Indian woman, the responsible daughter of an irresponsible woman. You—you make me feel right, too. And I felt it *so*

much it scared me. It still scares me because I could love
you so much. *So* much."

He grinned down at her. "There's that word again—
could."

"I…" she took a deep breath. "I do love you. You've
shown me what a man can be—not someone cruel, not
someone who comes and goes. A man who'll stay, who'll
do the right thing even if it's hard. Even if…"

"Even if it scares me. Like taking a baby home with
me." He took a step in and touched his forehead to hers.
"I hired the Polish grandmother, by the way. She's very
efficient. Just so we're clear—I'm not asking you to be a
nanny. I'm asking you to be my wife." He grinned. "My
permanent wife."

"Oh, Nate." She kissed him then, a light touching of
the lips.

He wrapped his arms around her and held her tight.
Suddenly, everything that had been wrong about the past
few days was right again because Nate was here and she
was here and they were together. "I missed you," she whispered. "I was already thinking about calling you after I
made it home."

He squeezed her tighter. "I couldn't wait that long. I
couldn't let you go without knowing exactly how much I
need you. I want you to come back to us because you know
that you belong with me."

"Yes," she whispered. "You're right. Loving you doesn't
mean I lose myself. I feel like, for the first time, I've *found*
myself."

He tilted her head back and stared into her eyes. "I'm
already yours, Trish Hunter. Will you be mine?"

This was what she wanted. To know that love wouldn't
destroy her like it always had her mother, to know that Nate

would fight for her. For them. "I'm yours, too. You're the only man I ever want."

He kissed her then, full of passion and promises. "Come home," he said when the kiss ended. "Sleep in my bed with me. And tomorrow we'll work on getting you out to the rez, okay? That's the plan."

"Tomorrow," she agreed. "But tonight…"

He kissed her again. "Tonight is ours."

That was a promise she knew he'd keep.

* * * * *

If you loved THE NANNY PLAN,
pick up Sarah M. Anderson's
A MAN OF DISTINCTION

A wealthy Native American lawyer must choose
between winning the case of his career and
reuniting with the love he left behind—and the
child she kept a secret.

Available now from Harlequin Desire!

And don't miss the next
BILLIONAIRES AND BABIES *story,*
TRIPLE THE FUN
from USA TODAY *bestselling author*
Maureen Child
Available May 2015!

If you're on Twitter, tell us what you think of
Harlequin Desire! #harlequindesire

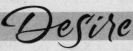
#2371 TRIPLE THE FUN
Billionaires and Babies • by Maureen Child
Nothing will stand between Connor and his triplets, not even their stubborn, sexy guardian. But Dina wants to raise the babies on her terms, even if it means resisting the most domineering—and desirable—man she's ever met.

#2372 MINDING HER BOSS'S BUSINESS
Dynasties: The Montoros • by Janice Maynard
Alex is on a royal mission for his country's throne. But when his assistant cozies up to a prince, unexpected jealously forces Alex to reevaluate his ideas about separating work from play...

#2373 KISSED BY A RANCHER
Lone Star Legends • by Sara Orwig
Josh seeks shelter at Abby's B&B...and gets snowed in! When they share a moonlit kiss, legend says it will lead to love. But can a cautious, small-town girl and a worldly Texas rancher turn myth into real romance?

#2374 THE SHEIKH'S PREGNANCY PROPOSAL
by Fiona Brand
After risking one passionate night with a sheikh, Sarah dismisses her dreams for a relationship—until her lover finds out she's pregnant. Suddenly, the rules change, because Gabe *must* marry the mother of his child!

#2375 SECRET HEIRESS, SECRET BABY
At Cain's Command • by Emily McKay
When Texas tycoon Grant Shepard seduced the lost Cain heiress, he ultimately walked away to protect her from her conniving family. But now she's back...and with a little secret that changes everything.

#2376 SEX, LIES AND THE CEO
Chicago Sons • by Barbara Dunlop
To prove the Colborns stole her late father's invention, Darci Rivers goes undercover at Colborn Aerospace—and even starts dating her billionaire boss! Can a double deception lead to an honest shot at happiness?

REQUEST YOUR FREE BOOKS!
2 FREE NOVELS PLUS 2 FREE GIFTS!

H HARLEQUIN® *Desire*

ALWAYS POWERFUL, PASSIONATE AND PROVOCATIVE

YES! Please send me 2 FREE Harlequin Desire® novels and my 2 FREE gifts (gifts are worth about $10). After receiving them, if I don't wish to receive any more books, I can return the shipping statement marked "cancel." If I don't cancel, I will receive 6 brand-new novels every month and be billed just $4.55 per book in the U.S. or $4.99 per book in Canada. That's a savings of at least 13% off the cover price! It's quite a bargain! Shipping and handling is just 50¢ per book in the U.S. and 75¢ per book in Canada.* I understand that accepting the 2 free books and gifts places me under no obligation to buy anything. I can always return a shipment and cancel at any time. Even if I never buy another book, the two free books and gifts are mine to keep forever.

225/326 HDN F4ZC

Name _____ (PLEASE PRINT) _____

Address _____ Apt. # _____

City _____ State/Prov. _____ Zip/Postal Code _____

Signature (if under 18, a parent or guardian must sign) _____

Mail to the Harlequin® Reader Service:
IN U.S.A.: P.O. Box 1867, Buffalo, NY 14240-1867
IN CANADA: P.O. Box 609, Fort Erie, Ontario L2A 5X3

Want to try two free books from another line?
Call 1-800-873-8635 or visit www.ReaderService.com.

* Terms and prices subject to change without notice. Prices do not include applicable taxes. Sales tax applicable in N.Y. Canadian residents will be charged applicable taxes. Offer not valid in Quebec. This offer is limited to one order per household. Not valid for current subscribers to Harlequin Desire books. All orders subject to credit approval. Credit or debit balances in a customer's account(s) may be offset by any other outstanding balance owed by or to the customer. Please allow 4 to 6 weeks for delivery. Offer available while quantities last.

Your Privacy—The Harlequin® Reader Service is committed to protecting your privacy. Our Privacy Policy is available online at www.ReaderService.com or upon request from the Harlequin Reader Service.

We make a portion of our mailing list available to reputable third parties that offer products we believe may interest you. If you prefer that we not exchange your name with third parties, or if you wish to clarify or modify your communication preferences, please visit us at www.ReaderService.com/consumerchoice or write to us at Harlequin Reader Service Preference Service, P.O. Box 9062, Buffalo, NY 14269. Include your complete name and address.

HD13R

SPECIAL EXCERPT FROM

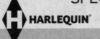

Desire

*Alex Ramon is all business when he's tasked with
restoring his country's royal family to the throne.
But when his sexy assistant cozies up to a prince,
his unexpected jealousy requires him to mix work
with pleasure…*

Read on for a sneak peek at
MINDING HER BOSS'S BUSINESS
the passionate first installment in the
DYNASTIES: THE MONTOROS series!

When a small orchestra launched into their first song,
Alex stood and held out his hand. "Do you feel like
dancing?"

He knew it was a tactical error as soon as he took
Maria in his arms. Given the situation, he'd assumed
dancing was a socially acceptable way to pass the time.

He was wrong. Dead wrong. No matter the public
venue or the circumspect way in which he held her, nothing could erase the fact that Maria was soft and warm in
his embrace. The slick fabric of her dress did nothing to
disguise the skin beneath.

He found his breath caught in his throat, lodged there
by a sharp stab of hunger. He'd worked so hard these past
weeks he'd let his personal needs slide. Celibacy was
neither smart nor sustainable. Certainly not when faced
daily with such deliciously carnal temptation.

When he couldn't think of a good reason to let her

go, one dance turned into three. Inevitably, his body responded to her nearness.

He was in heaven and hell, shuddering with arousal and unable to do a thing about it.

When the potential future prince brushed past them, his petite sister in his arms, Alex remembered what he had meant to say earlier. "Maria…"

"Hmm?"

Her voice had the warm, honeyed sound of a woman pleasured by her lover. Alex cleared his throat. "You need to be careful around Gabriel Montoro."

Maria's reaction was unmistakable. She went rigid and pulled away. "Excuse me?" Beautiful eyes glared at him.

Alex soldiered on. "He's a mature, experienced man, and you are very young. I'd hate to see him take advantage of you."

Maria went pale but for two spots of hectic color on her cheekbones. "Your concern is duly noted," she said, the words icy. "But you'll have to trust my judgment, I'm afraid."

Find out if Alex heeds Maria's advice (hint: he doesn't!)
in MINDING HER BOSS'S BUSINESS
by USA TODAY *bestselling author*
Janice Maynard.
Available May 2015 wherever
Harlequin Desire books and ebooks are sold

www.Harlequin.com

THE WORLD IS BETTER WITH

Romance

Harlequin has everything from contemporary, passionate and heartwarming to suspenseful and inspirational stories.

Whatever your mood, we have a romance just for you!

Connect with us to find your next great read, special offers and more.

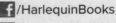

f /HarlequinBooks

🐦 @HarlequinBooks

www.HarlequinBlog.com

www.Harlequin.com/Newsletters

ⓗ HARLEQUIN®

A *Romance* FOR EVERY MOOD™

www.Harlequin.com